THE
LIST

The Secret Service: Agent Wayne Mitchell

CRAIG D. MCLAREN

Eagle Lost
Book One

The List
Book Two

The Secret Service: Agent Wayne Mitchell
BOOK 2

THE LIST

CRAIG D. MCLAREN

OAKTARA

WATERFORD, VIRGINIA

The List

Published in the U.S. by:
OakTara Publishers
P.O. Box 8
Waterford, VA 20197

Visit OakTara at
www.oaktara.com

Cover design by Muses9 Design
Cover image, jet © iStockphoto.com/sharply_done
Author photo © 2010 by Camy McLaren

ISBN: 978-1-60290-188-9

To all of the readers of *Eagle Lost,*
a grateful thank you.
The List is for you—
and all the new fans of the series.

And again,
thank you to
MY WONDERFUL WIFE,
CAMY.

One

Air Force 2

"O'Hare, this is Air Force 2 requesting clearance for landing." The pilot, Captain Chris Hogh, calmly converses with the control tower of O'Hare International Airport in Chicago on this clear warm night in late September.

"Roger, Air Force 2," the controller responds, "You are cleared for runway 2 nine-er. Winds are north/northwest at 12 miles per hour with gusts of 20 miles per hour."

"Roger that O'Hare," Captain Hogh answers while checking his instrumentation as he prepares the plane for final approach. He then addresses copilot Ingrid Fisher. "Prepare the crew for landing."

"Yes Captain." Ingrid turns on the intercom and announces that the flight crew should prepare for landing.

The O'Hare control tower personnel continue to monitor the approach of Air Force 2, which has Vice-President, Dave Charles, and chief of staff, Scott Bender, on board.

Then, all of a sudden, the controller hears, "Oh no!" from Captain Hogh.

The control room comes to a stop as everyone turns to listen. The silence is excruciating. Seconds pass before the controller notices that

1

Air Force 2 is showing a dramatic drop in altitude.

"Air Force 2, pull up, pull up," the controller firmly instructs the pilot. "You are coming in too steep."

There is no response from the pilot. Air Force 2 continues a rapid, near vertical descent.

"Pull up, pull up!" the controller tells Air Force 2…but gets no response.

The tower supervisor calls the airport fire department to prepare for a crash. Within seconds, sirens and lights converge on runway 29.

Back in the control tower, the air traffic controller and the rest of the tower personnel watch in horror as Air Force 2 drops off the screen and explodes in a huge ball of reddish orange light, shaking the tower.

Silence overtakes the room briefly as disbelief settles in. A second later, there is a mad rush of activity as years of training take over.

About 700 miles away in the White House, a state dinner is in progress in the State Dining Room, as President Bill Anders and his wife, Claire, host the British Prime Minister, along with many members of Congress and some celebrities. The dinner has been a great opportunity for the President to make his way among the tables to thank the Prime Minister and those members of Congress who have provided so much support to him. As he returns to the head table, his eye catches Diana Woodworth, a senior advisor, motioning to him. The President excuses himself and walks over to her. As he gets closer, he knows instantly that something is bothering her.

"Diana, what's the problem?" the President asks with a show of concern.

"Mr. President, would you follow me please? An urgent matter requires your attention."

Diana turns quickly and leaves the room with the President following close behind. Once they are out of the hearing range of the participants at the dinner, the aide addresses the President again.

"Sir, I have some terrible news. Air Force 2 just went down. It's feared that all on board are dead."

At first the President is speechless…in shock. Then, "Not Dave and Scott!"

"Sir," Diana says, "we need to address the press soon. Would you like me to prepare a statement with the press secretary?"

The President, still stunned by the news, hesitates. "No, Scott was one of my oldest and dearest friends. And Dave—" The President stares blankly for a moment. Then he refocuses. "Diana, I'll handle it myself."

Diana understands the decision but worries that the President may not be able to compose himself enough to address the press and the nation without losing control of his emotions. She asks the President if he feels okay.

"I'm fine," he says gently. "Please inform the guests after the First Lady and I leave."

He then walks back to the dinner to ask the First Lady and Mrs. Charles, the Vice President's wife, to come with him. Once they are out of the room, Diana begins to inform the guests of the tragedy.

The President leads the First Lady and Dave's wife, Lynn, up to the private quarters. Once upstairs he makes sure both are seated. Then, no longer feeling Presidential, Bill kneels in front of Lynn and holds her hand as he begins to tell her what happened. A loud cry goes through the private chambers, as Claire leans over to console Lynn, who sobs uncontrollably. Bill hugs them both for a long time. Then he stands up and heads downstairs to inform the nation.

The news of the death of the Vice-President, Dave Charles, and the chief of staff, Scott Bender, stuns the country. It will take a while for a complete analysis of the crash site and the "black box" that records the final moments of the activity in the cockpit, but preliminary reports of the wind gusts that were as high as twenty miles an hour may have caused a wind shear, says the news reports. Wind shear—a change in wind speed and/or direction within a short distance that causes a shearing or tearing effect—is the cause of many crashes. It always creates great concern for pilots, especially during takeoffs and landings.

When the President had addressed the nation announcing the crash and deaths, he'd asked the media personally to give the families privacy during their time of grief. Every one of them respected the request. But the President himself hadn't been able to honor it.

During his address, he had already sent one of his Secret Service Agents to search Bender's office in the White House for something the chief of staff had kept and maintained since the President's early days in politics. But it wasn't in Bender's office. Strange, since the President and Bender had always agreed that the item would be stored in a safe place. The President didn't fear it was lost in the plane crash, since neither of them carried it—doing so would leave open the possibility of it being lost or stolen. But he'd hoped it was in Bender's office. The agent, however, assured the President that he'd gone through everything—the item wasn't to be found.

The next day the President makes a special visit to the homes of Lynn Charles and her two lovely daughters, Angela and Jessica, and to Kathy Bender and their beautiful daughter, Taylor, who were not able to make the state dinner the night of the crash.

The President is becoming desperate. He has to find that item. If a political enemy—or worse, the media—find it, the fallout will be disastrous. *It has to be at Bender's home,* the President thinks. He wishes he could wait a respectful amount of time before asking Kathy about searching her home for it, but he anguishes over every minute he doesn't have it in his possession. Tomorrow morning he'll send an old friend to the Bender home to put Kathy at ease.

Two

Close to the First Family

Secret Service Agent Wayne Mitchell has been very busy the past year. He has overseen the investigation concerning the infiltration of our military and public officials by certain Russian emissaries while still serving the security needs of the First Family. Mitchell's long and personal history with them has given him a trust level rarely attained. While agents sometimes become very close with those they protect, when an agent has done what Agent Mitchell has done, a special bond is forged.

First, Agent Mitchell saved the then Senator's daughter, Amy, from being kidnapped. In addition, last year before the election, Agent Mitchell not only rescued the President from certain death, but also stopped the takeover of certain military and government operations by Russian agents who had been planning a sabotage of our military readiness for twenty years. This is what made Agent Mitchell special to the First Family. On top of all that, prior to protecting the President, he had been the agent assigned to protect chief of staff, Scott Bender.

Wayne Mitchell, now 31 years old, has been a Secret Service Agent for six years after joining the Agency straight from the military where he held the rank of Captain in the Marines. During that time he had stopped the kidnapping of Senator Anders' daughter. That, along with an exemplary military record, allowed him to find immediate acceptance. Soon he was protecting Bender.

At 6 feet 3 inches and a sculptured physique of 210 pounds, Agent Mitchell is an imposing figure. Add rugged handsome features, and you know why there isn't a female in Washington who wouldn't want him guarding her. After Bender's first wife died five years ago of cancer, there had been some murmurings amongst the "Washington crowd" that his new wife was a little young. At the time, Scott Bender was 54, and his blond-haired daughter, Taylor, was 13. His new wife, Kathy, was a 28-year-old blond beauty and at 5 feet 8 inches, could have been mistaken for a model. Everyone felt they knew why Scott had married her—it was not for her motherly instincts.

Wayne's assignment to Bender had only lasted about four months when his first wife died. It had devastated all who knew her, but mostly her daughter. With the age and personality difference of her new stepmother, Taylor struggled to accept Kathy as any type of authority figure. With her dad being away so much due to his being the chief of staff of a newly elected President, emotions and nerves became strained amongst the three of them. Many times Taylor dreamed of running away, but having a Secret Service Agent following her every move kept that from being an option.

Realizing Taylor's delicate emotional situation at the time, Bender had requested that the Secret Service reassign Wayne to Taylor and Taylor's agent to him. He felt that with Agent Mitchell's younger age of 26 at the time, he might be able to communicate somewhat with his daughter. He realized it was a stretch, but one that was worth taking. Over time it became a good decision, at least as Taylor was concerned, for she eventually developed a crush on Wayne. For Wayne, it was a little trickier since he was there to protect her. Deep down Taylor realized that too, but it still did not stop her from fantasizing about the great life they would have together someday.

There was another problem: the close working relationship of Wayne and Bender's new wife, Kathy. Even though they maintained a very professional relationship, they could not stop the rumors that eventually started. With the closeness of their ages and being together so often, it became an under-the-breath discussion amongst other agents and some of Bender's staff. It didn't take long for Scott to hear them.

Not wanting to give the rumors any credence, for he trusted Kathy and Wayne without question, he initially did his best to ignore them. For a while, the talk seemed to dissipate, but he would hear something occasionally that would bring back the disturbing images of possibility in his mind. He decided that when Taylor left for college, he would switch the agents back and have Wayne with him from then on.

All too soon Taylor was on her way to college and Wayne was back guarding the chief of staff, but his closeness with Taylor and Kathy was always there. A year after that, after saving the President's life, Wayne was assigned to a special task force where his primary duties revolved around the President.

Even though Wayne is no longer protecting the chief of staff, news of Bender's death affects him deeply. He's anxious to give his heartfelt condolences to Kathy and Taylor. Over the last year, Taylor and Kathy have at last become closer and supportive of each other, something they both will need a lot of now. They still have the same mother-daughter problems most have, but the resentment Taylor initially felt has changed to the belief that Kathy truly loves her.

Today Wayne is supposed to give a presentation to the joint chiefs concerning final recommendations for addressing weaknesses in certain fail-safe measures that had failed during last year's attempt at sabotaging our military readiness. But with the deaths of both the Vice-President and chief of staff, the meeting is postponed until next week.

Instead he receives an early call from the White House to come immediately. When he arrives, he is ushered to the Oval Office, where the President, somewhat agitated, paces the floor. When Wayne enters, the President extends his hand in greeting.

"Glad you could get here on such short notice," the President says. "I know I may have taken you from something very important, but once I tell you my problem, I'm sure you'll appreciate my need for you to get here."

"No problem, Mr. President. I hope I can help."

The President motions Wayne to sit in one of the chairs positioned in front of his desk as he walks around the desk to sit in his chair.

The President takes a moment to collect his thoughts before beginning. "Wayne, as you know, two great public servants were lost to the American people."

Wayne nods.

"As you also know, Scott was a long-time friend of mine, going all the way back to our days at the University of Wisconsin."

Wayne nods again.

"What you don't know is that he was also the keeper of a list—the names of many powerful people. These people, mostly in our government, but also from other governments, have supplied me many favors over my many years in government service. I have also returned those favors over those same years. Some of the favors might not reflect positively on those involved or this administration if they would become known."

President Anders waits a moment, as if to judge Wayne's reaction, but Wayne, straight-faced, continues to sit quietly, intent on listening.

"In order for Scott and me to maintain a continuing knowledge of these favors and their history, Scott kept a list of each one," the President said. "It is in code, but it describes the favor—when it was given and for whom. The code, though, is low tech, consisting of names that follow the hurricane name list of the year for the favor given. Early on, it was all female names, until the National Hurricane Center switched to alternating male and female names in 1979. We never really put a lot of thought into the best way to do it. We were young, and we just did it the first way we thought of. I'm embarrassed to say the code words used to represent the favors were types of male-female encounters. We thought it funny at the time.

"We fully believed that these favors were done to provide not only a better America, but also a better world. And as we continued in our political ambitions, we found that this was the way to get things done not only in Washington, but throughout the world. I'd like to be able to say I would change how these favors came to be, but in actuality, they have accomplished many great things. True, a few did not turn out as envisioned, but the vast majority did."

Wayne tries not to react as if the President has said something out of the ordinary, but inside he's disturbed. Here is a man he greatly admires, telling him that over many years he and Scott Bender have been trading favors for what they feel is for the betterment of America and the world. Now he wants Wayne to do something for him. *Obviously, he's not talking the small favors we all did for each other as kids, so what does he want from me?* Wayne wonders.

"I'd hoped that the list had been left in Scott's office here in the West Wing, but I had another agent scour it, and he could not find it."

"Could it have been lost in the plane crash?" Wayne asks.

"No, we always maintained the rule that we would never carry the list with us for fear of losing it or having it stolen. There is only one place left it can be, and I need you to go there and retrieve it."

"Where would that be, sir?"

"At Scott's home."

The color temporarily leaves Wayne's face.

"I know this may cause you some discomfort," the President acknowledges, "but you are the only one I feel can accomplish this with the least amount of trouble. Your history with the family will allow you to visit the home with a minimum amount of interest by the media. Since you were assigned to both Scott and Taylor in the past, it will look like a condolence visit. The funeral isn't for a few days—to allow dignitaries time to make the trip here—and the press has agreed to stay away from the residence until after the funeral. You should be able to make your visit and return without much interference. Obviously, the need to keep your assignment quiet goes without saying."

Wayne nods in understanding. He thinks about reminding the President of all the rumors concerning Bender's wife, Kathy, and him, but decides against it. He knows the President is counting on him.

"I'll see to it, Mr. President," Wayne states firmly. "What does the ledger look like?"

"Like your typical black book," the President answers with a smirk. "About the size of a small paperback novel. Once you open it, you'll be able to tell if you have it."

Wayne again nods and gets up to leave. The President gets up with him and makes his way around his desk to walk Wayne to the door.

"Wayne, once again I owe you," the President states. Wayne smiles and leaves the Oval Office.

Three

The True Purpose

At about 10:20 a.m., Wayne starts his drive to the Bender residence after first calling Kathy to make sure she'll be there and that it will be all right to stop by. She sounds pleased that he wants to visit and adds that Taylor will be pleased to see him too. He hopes that when he explains the true purpose of the visit, their feelings don't change.

He also had to cancel his 1 p.m. golf game with a good friend and fellow agent Austin Ivers, telling him he'll make it up with dinner at one of their favorite restaurants. Ivers had been the agent assigned to protect former President Shane Osburn, while he was President. After Osburn lost the reelection bid, Agent Ivers chose to stay in Washington and serve where needed instead of continuing with the former President. Being of the opposition party that now occupies the White House, Wayne, for the last few years, has been kidding Austin about his not protecting the "Main Man" anymore. Therefore, they take their little battle out to the golf course once a week.

As he drives to meet with the Benders, he calls Jackson 20, a great restaurant located in the Hotel Monaco, just on the other side of the Potomac in Old Town Alexandria, Virginia. The restaurant takes its name from Andrew Jackson, whose face is on the twenty-dollar bill. Wayne makes the dinner reservation for 5 p.m. to beat the dinner rush. It'll give him plenty of time to spend with the Benders and do what the

President has asked of him.

It takes about an hour to get to the Bender residence from the White House. Scott had built a beautiful compound in Delaware for his family five years ago after the death of his first wife. He did not want Kathy having to deal with any ghost of the past, and he needed to give his family a secure and private environment away from all the prying eyes of Washington. Even the closest neighbor is over a mile away. After getting off Highway 50/301 once you enter Delaware, you go about a mile south before coming to the entrance gate that gives you access to Bender Lane. At the end of this lane is a large finger of land formed by waterways that eventually flow past Shaw Bay, then Eastern Bay, and eventually empty into the Chesapeake Bay.

As Wayne's car approaches the entrance gate to the road to the home, he's surprised there are no media trucks around, waiting for an opportunity to record any type of activity that might result in a story. Then he remembers the President's request that all media respect the privacy of the families during this national time for grieving. Wayne is impressed that the media has kept the President's trust.

After entering the code Kathy gave him to the gate, Wayne pulls into the Bender drive that meanders about a half mile through a beautiful park-like setting and past a large guest house before reaching the front of the main house where Wayne parks his car. Again, no press. He hesitates for a moment to get his thoughts together, then opens the car door.

He's barely out of his car when the front door of the house opens. Out of the corner of his eye, he sees Taylor running to him with open arms. She rushes to him and they give each other a warm hug. Taylor presses her head into Wayne's chest; he can tell she is crying. They hold each other for a few more seconds, then slowly pull away. Taylor looks up into his face. Wayne can see she has become a beautiful young woman with long blond hair, piercing blue eyes, and a face that will break many hearts over the years.

"Thanks for coming, Wayne," Taylor speaks through her tears.

Wayne smiles into her eyes. He puts his arm around her shoulders and walks with her back into the house. Wayne always liked the very homey feeling he got from the Bender home when he worked here, and

12

he still feels it. The house is traditional with a formal entrance and foyer and the main staircase directly in your view when you enter. To the left is Scott Bender's office and to the right, the formal living room. Behind the main staircase is the kitchen with the formal dining room to the left of that. Straight back of the kitchen is the family room with bar and entertainment area. Just off the back of the living room, through some French doors, the beautiful covered patio is always perfectly decorated with flowers of the season.

As Wayne and Taylor enter the home, Kathy is sitting in the living room. She motions for them to come over and sit on the couch facing her.

"Wayne! How good to see you again," Kathy says with the sweet voice Wayne remembers. "I'm so pleased you could drop by."

"I wanted to come by earlier, but I also wanted to give you some time." Wayne forces the truth out of his mouth, but with his additional purpose, it leaves a bitter taste.

Kathy nods. "That's understandable. We actually requested that our friends and relatives give us a couple of days to ourselves to sort things out, but when you called we agreed it would be good for us to spend some time with a very good friend."

"So no one is staying in the guest house?" Wayne asks.

"No."

At first Wayne thinks of delaying confessing the additional reason for the visit, but he doesn't want to mislead them any more than he has to. He looks down for a moment then begins.

"As much as I wish this visit was for the sole reason of sitting down with both of you and enjoying each other's company today," Wayne says slowly, "the President requested I come and ask a big favor of you both."

Kathy and Taylor looked confused.

"What favor would that be, Wayne?" Kathy says with slightly less sweetness than before.

"Scott maintained something very private that is important to national security. The President believes he kept it here," Wayne explains. "Would you allow me to look through his effects to see if it is amongst them?"

Kathy considers Wayne coldly. "Obviously I'm disappointed that's why you are here, but if you and the President feel so strongly that this item is of such national security that it couldn't wait until after we at least have a chance to put Scott to rest, then by all means rummage through his things."

Kathy's voice starts breaking up as she finishes her answer. Then she begins sobbing, and her head falls into her hands.

Wayne feels terrible for not being here for the reason they had hoped. They are friends, and he has bruised that friendship. He can now only hope that time will allow it to heal. Wayne gets up from the couch as Taylor moves over to Kathy to hold her. Wayne walks out of the living room, across the entrance hall, and over to Scott's den, where his desk is.

For the better half of an hour, he goes through everything in and on the desk, plus on the bookshelves. There is no ledger. Wayne, frustrated and angry that he will now have to ask if he can go through Scott and Kathy's bedroom, sits down in Scott's chair to think out how he is going to ask this of Kathy. Leaning back in the chair, he stares across the room and out the den window.

It's then that he notices that a black, late-model sedan has parked near his car. Wayne gets out of Scott's chair and quickly makes his way to the entrance hall just as a knock sounds on the front door.

He sees Taylor moving toward the door and motions for her to stand still. "Are either of you expecting anyone?" he whispers to Taylor and Kathy.

They shake their heads no. At that moment, Wayne wonders where the Secret Service Agents assigned to Kathy and Taylor are and why there was no access request ring from the front gate.

Wayne tells Taylor to go back into the living room, then opens the door. Standing at the door's entrance is a large man about 6 feet 5 inches, weighing about 260 pounds, and wearing very dark sunglasses.

"May I help you?" Wayne asks the large man.

The man seems startled at who opened the door. In the split second that Wayne waits for the man to answer, he sees a reflection off the man's sunglasses of another man leaning against the house just out of sight. Wayne quickly slams the door shut and bolts it. He then dives into the living room as gunshots start shredding the area around the doorknob and bolt.

Wayne pulls Kathy and Taylor down to the floor with him and behind the couch.

The front door shatters from the force of the 260 pound man crashing through it. Wayne pulls his gun from its holster and aims at the man, dropping him with two well-placed shots to his chest. The second attacker dives through the entrance hall and slides behind the wall separating it from the living room. A second later, he is shooting around the wall at Wayne. Not wanting to continue to exchange gunfire while Kathy and Taylor lay next to him, Wayne looks around the room for a way out. The French doors leading out to the backyard are the only option.

Just then the man behind the wall yells out. "You can walk away from this. All I'm here for is something from Bender's desk. Throw your gun out, and once I locate what I'm here for, I will leave."

Is this person looking for the same thing I came for? Wayne wonders. One thing for sure, he isn't going to give up his gun.

Wayne whispers to Kathy and Taylor, "We're going through those French doors. I am going to shoot a couple of rounds at him while I run to them. You both follow right on my heels. Do not stop for anything, understand?"

Kathy and Taylor nod to show they understand. Wayne quietly says, "Now!" to let them know to start running, then stands up and fires four rounds in the direction of the attacker. Kathy and Taylor follow closely behind Wayne as he runs toward the French doors, firing twice more at the man behind the wall. When Wayne reaches the doors, he braces himself and throws his shoulder into them, causing the doors to shatter and fly out to the patio and backyard beyond. Kathy and Taylor run through the now open doors and continue running with Wayne to the back of the house.

Wayne waits for a second to make sure the attacker isn't following, then leads Kathy and Taylor behind the utility shed, about 40 yards from the back of the house. "Stay here," he urges them, then cautiously makes his way back to the house. Quietly he runs to the outside wall of the family room and hugs it until he gets to where the French doors used to be hanging. With his gun ready, he pokes his head through the opening and listens. He can hear Scott's desk drawers opening, closing, and the rustling of papers. Wayne heads into the house.

He's certain of one thing: This man looking through Bender's desk has only one purpose—to find and recover something. He isn't going to be distracted into following Wayne and the Benders. He's probably glad they're gone, because he wasn't looking forward to killing them...something he'd probably have had to do had they surrendered. Frustration, though, is setting in, as he cannot find what he is looking for. His determination to locate the item has left him vulnerable to Wayne's return. As the man straightens up from searching in the last bottom drawer of the desk, Wayne stands in the doorway, pointing a gun at his head.

"Who sent you?" Wayne demands.

The man smiles, realizing Wayne is more than just a visiting friend of the family. Now he knows he should have followed them out of the house and killed them.

"You know I'm not going to tell you that," the man points out. "But give me what I'm looking for, and this can all end right now."

Wayne smiles back. "What would it be you're looking for?"

"Come on," the man flung back, irritated. "If I don't come back with it, more will come and the chance your friends will live through it will drop drastically."

Wayne reacts calmly to the man's threat. "Again, I'll ask. What are you looking for?"

The man shakes his head, then blurts out, "Bender's Ledger."

"What do you know about his ledger?" Wayne challenges the man.

"Me? Not much, but my boss knows a lot about it."

"And who would your boss be?"

The man only smiles.

"Well," Wayne begins, "I guess we'll just go back to my office to discuss this a little more."

"No," the man corrects Wayne. "You have got two choices: Let me go or kill me. If you let me go, I'll go back to my boss and tell him I couldn't find it. Maybe he will give up the search. If you kill me, your friends will never have another peaceful day until he finds it."

16

Wayne knows the man is right about one thing. He won't let himself be taken in for any type of interrogation. His manner and demeanor shows he is a highly trained operative. He made one mistake though; he let Wayne come back.

The intruder does not wait long for an answer, though. His hand moves quickly to his gun lying on the desk.

But Wayne is quicker. One shot later and the intruder is dead with a bullet just above the right eye. Wayne would have preferred wounding him and getting some usable information out of him, but as the man moved to his gun he stooped, trying to get below the top of the desk. Wayne couldn't let that happen, so took the kill shot.

After confirming the man is dead, Wayne heads out to the shed to get his friends.

Four

A Dangerous Situation

After Wayne brings Kathy and Taylor back into the living room, he asks questions about what has now become a dangerous situation. "First, where are the Secret Service Agents assigned to you both?"

Kathy looks puzzled. "They were taken away yesterday. They said they had been reassigned since Scott was no longer alive, and we had been taken off the watch list."

Wayne has trouble believing the reassignment of the agents would happen so quickly. It's true that Kathy and Taylor's agent needs left with Scott's passing, but this is too soon for it to happen. Something's definitely wrong.

"Taylor," Wayne calmly begins, "I want you to go upstairs and pack just what you need for a few days."

Taylor nods and heads upstairs.

When Taylor is out of sight, Wayne turns to Kathy. "Are you aware of a ledger that Scott kept over the years?"

Kathy shakes her head.

"Well," Wayne begins his explanation, "Scott maintained a special list for many years, and it's now apparent that it's no longer a secret. I need to get you and Taylor out of here and to a safe location. There's no telling how many people know of this list and are willing to come after you for it, so go get just what you need and I'll get you to a safe location until we can figure this out."

Kathy, looking scared and confused, heads upstairs while Wayne makes his way back to Scott's office to make a call. As he picks up the phone and lifts it to his ear, he immediately knows there's a problem. Not only is there no dial tone, but outside he doesn't see the black car anymore. He's been as stupid as the man he just killed. In all the activity, Wayne has failed to confirm there were only two attackers. Because of this, he has left his friends in danger. He quickly remembers seeing Bender's gun and extra ammunition in the desk. He grabs them, then makes his way upstairs to the Kathy and Taylor. Their doors are open, and he can see they are still in the process of packing.

"Kathy, Taylor," Wayne calls out firmly, "we do not have any more time. Grab what you have and come with me."

They both close their bags and head with Wayne down the stairs and to the front door of the house. Just as they reach the front door, a loud voice is heard from outside.

"Those in the house come out now, and no harm will come to you. Stay in there, and you will leave us no other choice but to kill you."

Wayne motions for Kathy and Taylor to stay low and out of sight as he makes his way to the side of the window that looks out to the front yard from Scott's office. He can't see who is speaking, but he now sees the black car has come back, plus two more. Wayne motions for Kathy and Taylor to stay where they are while he makes his way to the living room on the other side of the entranceway so he can try seeing out those windows. There are two windows facing the front yard plus one window on each side of the fireplace on the side of the house. Decorative drapes frame all four windows with blinds to block out the sun.

Wayne stays low as he moves to the side window just right of the fireplace. Very slowly he uses his index finger to separate a couple of the slats. What he sees startles him. In addition to the four vehicles out front, there are three more to the side of the house, plus a large truck. Wayne reaches into his pocket and pulls out his cell phone. He pushes speed dial to Secret Service Headquarters. There is nothing but silence as Wayne checks the bars to indicate reception and sees none. He knows this is impossible since he's used a cell phone on many occasions during his time he was assigned to the Benders. He asks Kathy and Taylor to try their phones. They have the same result.

Wayne now knows there will be no calls to the outside. The cell phones are being jammed by portable jamming devices, probably CJ9As, around the house. These are capable of blocking all bands from 800MHz to 1900MHz within a 600-foot range by disrupting phone to tower frequencies using radio waves along the same frequencies that cellular phones use. The devices are more than adequate to keep calls from being sent or received.

Wayne puts on his brave face before he turns to Kathy and Taylor. He isn't afraid for himself but frustrated with the lack of protection he has provided them. He is desperate to protect them—this time not because it's what he is trained to do, but because they are his friends.

"Guys," Wayne begins, "we've been cut off from the outside."

Taylor gasps while Kathy holds her tightly.

Wayne continues, "I'm going to need you both to be very brave and do exactly what I say."

Both Kathy and Taylor nod.

"We can hold them off in here for quite a while if we need to," Wayne points out. "Both of you go upstairs and bring down the bed mattresses from yours and the spare bedrooms."

They quickly make their way up the stairs. Wayne continues to monitor the outside activity. So far, other than glimpses of a couple of people scurrying around the house, he has been unable to tell how many are out there.

A minute later Kathy and Taylor drag the mattresses down the stairs. With the arranging of the couch and some chairs he has some protection, but he needs to put the mattresses up where the front door and French doors used to be. They won't offer any real protection, but they will help to block the view of those trying to see in. While trying to stay out of the line of sight, Wayne positions the mattresses as best as he can over the openings of what is left of the front and French doors.

Wayne knows their situation is desperate. The people outside won't wait long before they try to breach what little fortification Wayne has set up. Those outside know that time is not on their side. It won't be long before someone tries to make a call to the house and questions why they can't get through. Initially they might think the Benders had turned their cell phones off and taken the phone off the hook for some privacy, but that would only buy a little additional time. For this reason, Wayne knows the intruders will soon attempt to enter the house. Again, Wayne hears the voice from outside.

"Those of you in the house," a voice calls, "I'm sure we all agree that you don't want to die. Moreover, to be honest, we'd rather not have to kill you. As you probably have already discovered, you have no outside communication ability. All we want is something that Mr. Bender has stored somewhere in the house. If you let us in, we'll just locate it and leave peacefully."

Wayne knows they are here for the same thing he is: the list. The man he just killed referred to it as "Bender's Ledger," but it has to be the same thing. Even if he could trust the man yelling from outside, there's no way Wayne can allow the list to fall into anyone's hands but the President's. Kathy and Taylor being here also make this a matter of protection, not just national security. His only hope is to make the intruders' attempt to enter the house as physically expensive to them as possible.

Five

Tension Runs High

Outside the Bender home, tension is running high. The eight men left to retrieve the list know they don't have much time before someone shows up, concerned about the Benders. They are especially concerned that there is someone else in there with them. Someone they were not expecting.

Garrett, the man who has been yelling into the house, snaps at Mo Mower, one of his associates. "What on earth do they think they can accomplish by staying in there?"

"I'm afraid they believe they'll be killed anyway," Mo bluntly points out. "Can you really expect anything else when the first two you send in start shooting their way into the house?"

Garrett glares at Mo, who, realizing his verbal mistake, turns and leaves. But Garrett has to admit he probably should have gone to the house himself. However, there shouldn't have been anyone home, except the two women, since the Secret Service Agents were not to be there. It's now obvious that the car at the front of the house doesn't belong to the Benders.

Garrett turns to one of the other men near him. "Call the office and see if anyone knows who might be in the house with the Bender women. I want to have all the information I can before we rush in this time. And take down the plate number on the vehicle in front of the house and see who it's assigned to."

The man nods and moves to a distance far enough away from the cell phone jamming devices placed around the house so he can make his call.

Garrett, like Wayne Mitchell, is a tall man of 6 feet 3 inches, but not as well built. His waist has been growing over the years as he's indulged in more of the foods and drinks he loves. He's also showing his older age in the graying around the temples, but even at 45, he's still a formidable person to deal with. Most of the time now, though, he sends his employees to do what jobs are required. But today he'd received an urgent call to give this matter his personal attention. Moreover, when this person requests Garrett Coffman, he expects Garrett Coffman.

A few minutes later, the man reports back to Garrett. "Sir, no one knows for sure how many are in the house with the women. The agents were taken away from the Benders as we thought, but we have another problem."

"What is it?" Garrett blurts out when the man hesitates too long.

"The office ran a check on the plates from the car." He hesitated. "They belong to Secret Service Agent Wayne Mitchell."

Garrett's face tightens and starts to lose its color. "What is he doing here?" Garrett questions the man.

"The office isn't quite sure, but he might only have been paying his condolences. So the potential good news is that he may be the only one in there with the women."

Garrett turns toward the house and shakes his head in disbelief at this turn of events. This is not what he had planned. He knows that even if it is only Wayne Mitchell, this will get ugly before it gets better. Wayne won't allow anyone into that house if he can prevent it.

"Go get Mo," Garrett tells the man.

"Yes sir." The man heads over to the other side of the house.

Mo Mower is Garrett's go-to man when the situation calls for someone who has no problem taking care of business by any means necessary. Most of the time Garrett doesn't care or even want to know what Mo does, he just knows the job will get done. Mo is not that big of a man, standing just 5 feet 10 inches and weighing in at 190 pounds, but what he has is all muscle. He looks younger than his age of 40 years, due to his well-kept, mid-length, sandy colored hair and light complexion. Just looking at him wouldn't disclose the evil that ran through his blood.

Garrett sees Mo coming from back of the house. When he reaches Garrett, there is a moment of silence as Garrett looks toward the house, then back to Mo. "I'm afraid I'm going to need your special talents on this one."

Mo jerks his head down and up, once.

"And this time it has to be done quickly. We can't let this situation last any longer."

"I understand, sir. It will be done as you ask."

Mo heads to where a few of the additional men are and motions them over to him.

Garrett doesn't like the way things have gone so far, but now it will end. His hope for a quick finish to the Benders and recovery of the list ended with the arrival of Wayne Mitchell. Mitchell would know there is no plan to let anyone leave the house alive.

Back in the house, Wayne is positioning himself for the best possible defense of the Benders. Realizing that the people trying to get in the house are professionals, he knows they won't try to burn them out. The large amount of smoke released into the air by such a fire would surely bring unwanted attention. No, they will have to find a way into the house. Normally a person would think that the safest place to go is to the basement—no windows and only one entrance to defend—but Wayne knows that would allow anyone coming into the house to trap them. They could throw fire, explosives, almost anything down the basement. He motions to Kathy and Taylor to make their way back upstairs. That will give Wayne a position of strength against anyone charging into the house. After positioning the couch and some of the chairs behind the mattresses placed against the broken doors, Wayne follows Kathy and Taylor up the stairs.

Upstairs there are three large bedrooms and a room that could have been a fourth bedroom but is Kathy's office. From there she oversees her charity work and the everyday requirements of the wife of the chief of staff for the President of the United States. Each bedroom has its own bathroom. Of the bedrooms, the master bedroom is located in the back of the house, directly over the family room, so its large windows can overlook the backyard garden.

Kathy's office, which partially cantilevers over the back patio, also gets views of the backyard garden. The other two bedrooms face the front of the house. There is a laundry room just to the left of the top of the stairs. The laundry room has the entrance to the attic. The attic lays over the whole upstairs, but the ceiling height of the attic lowers, as you get closer to the walls. The roof then tapers down on the sides.

Upstairs, Wayne sees that Taylor is crying as Kathy holds her. Wayne walks over and puts his arms around them, "I'm going to do everything I can to keep you both safe. I want you both to go into the laundry room and then up to the attic."

Both Kathy and Taylor head immediately to the laundry room as Wayne walks back to the stairs. He then hurries back down to the first floor to prepare for the inevitable. Wayne figures the attack will come from the already breached front and back doors, which only have mattresses keeping them out now. Knowing he has little time, he goes to the attached garage, which is to the left side of the family room through the mudroom, to see what he can find that may slow their eagerness to come into the house. Wayne sees what he hoped he would find in a garage of a large property owner: gasoline, flares, duct tape, a heavy metal rake, a pitchfork, and an extra box of ammunition for Bender's handgun.

Going back into the house, he stops in the kitchen to grab as many steak and carving knives as he can find. With everything in hand, he begins to prepare his greeting for anyone trying to get into the house uninvited. He skillfully positions the metal rake and pitchfork above the two broken doors, hanging with counter weights and attached to hair trigger latches to release with the slightest disturbance. He then tapes the flares to the two gasoline filled cans he found and positions them in the swing path of the rake and pitchfork so that when they are released, the force of the movement will strike the flare and ignite it, which in turn will ignite the gas cans.

Just because the people outside are not anxious to cause some smoke doesn't mean Wayne should not. The house, when built, had a commercial grade sprinkler system installed that goes on in the area where fire is detected. That would keep the fire from spreading and would extinguish it, but not until it had done its job. Wayne then goes back up to the top of the stairs, with his remaining arsenal of weapons, to wait. He looks at his watch: 1:12 p.m. It won't be long now.

Within five minutes there is a loud crash from the back French doors, followed by an even louder scream. Wayne knows the pitchfork has done its job. Only a couple of seconds pass and Wayne sees the front door mattress jolt forcibly into the house as the heavy metal rake shoots in a downward arc toward the man following the mattress in. The rake catches the man below the chin, penetrating the throat. The man squirms in pain, but the location of the punctures keeps the scream muffled. Wayne assumes that whoever came through the French doors were hit in the chest or face by the pitchfork from the loud scream.

All of a sudden, a loud explosion shakes the house from the area of the French doors as Wayne sees flames shoot below him. A second later the gas can at the front door does the same. Wayne sees the flames engulf the man impaled on the rake and cover the man following behind him. He quickly turns back away from the flames and starts to roll around in the grass out in front of the house. Wayne, carrying some of the knives he had brought from the kitchen, makes his way down the stairs as the sprinkler system kicks on.

Positioning one of the knives in his hand, Wayne, deftly throws it with pinpoint accuracy through the opening that was the front door, toward the squirming man on the front lawn, hitting him squarely in the back. The man stops his squirming. Wayne makes his way past the one caught on the rake as he gives him a precise stab with another knife, ending his suffering. The smoke is heavy in the house as the sprinklers continue to work to put out the fire, but Wayne can make out someone hanging from the pitchfork. It has gone straight through his face and the fire has overwhelmed him. He's no longer moving.

Wayne cautiously moves through the living room until he gets to the opening of the broken French doors. Outside he sees a couple of men helping another man; the flames from the gas can explosion obviously had hit him. Wayne has little time as he changes his grip on the knife. The position he's in doesn't allow for a normal throw, so planting his right foot, his arm swings across his body, as if he's throwing a Frisbee, and lets the knife go. One of the men helping the burned man drops to one knee as the blade of the knife penetrates his lower back. It slows the man only for a second as he quickly regains his footing. That, though, is all the time Wayne needs to get into a better position to throw one more knife. The man takes only a couple more steps before the second knife finds its mark in the middle of his back. The man slumps to the ground, then fully collapses. The burned man and second rescuer make their way out of sight before Wayne can do anything more.

As Wayne turns into the house, he sees that the flames are almost out. A large amount of smoke is escaping through the broken doors. For a quick second he thinks the fire department will be on its way since the fire alarm system is programmed to notify them whenever the sprinkler system activates, but in the same instance, he remembers the only way they are notified is through the phone line that has been cut. The smoke amount is substantial, but it will end soon. The sprinklers will shut off, leaving everything saturated and preventing any future ignition. The likelihood of any of the distant neighbors reacting to the smoke is remote, but those outside won't be able to take that chance. They'll have to do something.

Six

Disappointment

As the two men leave from the failed attempt to enter the Bender home return, Garrett Coffman grimaces in disappointment in what has transpired. This is the first time Mo has failed him and it doesn't sit well. He calms himself down before turning to Mo.

"Would you like to tell me why we are not inside the Bender home right now, retrieving the ledger?"

Mo understands there is no answer that will appease Coffman, so he just shakes his head. He knows Mitchell is a capable agent, but who would have guessed he'd risk burning the house with the two women inside? The one thing he did get out of this is the answer of how many men are with the Bender women—just one, Wayne. Moreover, since he didn't fire any shots, he might be out of ammunition.

Garrett doesn't wait for an answer. "How many men do we have stationed at the front gate?"

"Four sir."

"Send someone to bring two here, and let's hope those two are all we need to reinforce our perceived advantage. Tell the other two to be prepared to explain away any concerns about the smoke to inquisitive neighbors. And get me a phone; I need to make a call."

Back in the house, Wayne tries to identify the two dead men left inside, but both are burned beyond recognition. The dead men outside are, unfortunately, sprawled facedown and too far from the house. He places what's left of the charred mattresses back against the door openings to continue to block any views from the outside, then heads up the stairs. He feels he has a few moments before the intruders' next attempt. Upstairs he knocks on the attic door and calls out their names. Seconds later, the attic door opens, and he sees their relieved faces.

Mo returns to Garrett just as he is hanging up the phone. "The men are on their way up the road, sir," Mo reports.

"Fine. When they get here, bring them to me. I have a plan I want you to put into action."

"Yes, sir."

Back in the house, Wayne climbs the stairs into the attic. As soon as he is in, both Kathy and Taylor hug him tightly. Knowing they don't have much time, he regretfully breaks the embrace after a couple seconds.

"This isn't over yet," Wayne informs them.

He glances around the attic to see what Kathy and Taylor can use to defend themselves if needed. The usual attic stuff is immediately visible: old clothes, shoes, books, and plenty of boxes filled with memorabilia. However, his eyes lock on a corner filled with old sports gear and equipment. What's propped up against the wall will work perfectly. Wayne walks over to the corner, picks up two baseball bats, and hands them to Kathy and Taylor.

"I want you both to hang on to these. Unless you know it's me, swing first and ask questions later, understand?"

Both Kathy and Taylor nod, but a visibly shaken Taylor blurts out, "Why are they doing this to us?" then starts crying uncontrollably.

Kathy hugs her as Wayne tries to explain. "I think they're here to find something that can be used against our country, and it's my job to keep that from happening. As much as I wish I could believe them when they say they mean no harm, considering how quick they started shooting, that's probably a lie."

Taylor continues to cry as Kathy holds her even tighter.

"I'm sorry, but I've got to get back downstairs. Remember, swing first, *then* ask questions."

Kathy looks up from Taylor and nods. Wayne turns toward the attic door and begins to step down. He takes one last look back at his friends. Taylor breaks away from Kathy and grabs Wayne and holds on. Wayne puts his arms around her, trying his best to comfort her. But there simply isn't time. He squeezes tightly…and lets go. Taylor lets her arms fall and walks back to Kathy. They both watch as Wayne continues his descent to the second floor.

Outside, Garrett goes over a plan with Mo and the two men from the front gate that will take about an hour to put into place. It will be another attack to the front and back of the house simultaneously, but this time Mo will be a part of it—something Garrett had been disappointed was not part of the first attempt. Garrett will now use Mo the way he should have from the beginning. With the plan laid out, Mo begins to get things ready.

Down on the first floor of the house, Wayne starts planning his response options to various scenarios. None is a clear winner, but a couple make more sense. He prepares for what he feels is the most likely thing to happen. He decides to stay downstairs so he can be more mobile and sets up from Scott Bender's office. From there he can see most of the first floor. Through the office back door, he can see into the dining room, kitchen, and anyone coming in from the family room, but mainly he can see the front of the stairs going up to the second floor. At all costs, he will keep anyone from going up those stairs.

He takes a couple of knives with him and slips them in his belt, but feels they have already served their purpose of confusing the attackers on why he did not shoot at them this last time. It was more because he hadn't had the time to load Scott's gun than really anything else, but he's sure they are thinking he's out of bullets. That could initially work to his advantage.

He lays out Scott's handgun and extra ammo on the desk, then checks his gun. Good thing Scott had been smart enough to keep extra ammunition, Wayne, not planning on a shootout during this visit, knows he has only one .357 SIG cartridge left in the 10 round magazine for his SIG Sauer P229 pistol. However, Scott's classic Smith & Wesson Model 637 snub-nose .38 will do just fine. The two greatest strengths of this gun are its excellent accuracy and 13.5-ounce weight. Its exposed hammer allows it to be cocked for single-action fire. This makes for even greater accuracy.

The main setback, Wayne knows, is that even though a snub-nose .38 can launch a bigger bullet than any other pistol of its size and weight, a 158-grain slug, it can only send five of them before you have to reload. Wayne hopes the greater accuracy will reduce his need to reload too often as he shoves the five bullets into each chamber. He grabs a handful of extra ammo and shoves them into his pants pocket as he leans back in Scott's desk chair and waits.

Garrett looks at his watch. *2:43 p.m.* His plan won't be ready for at least another 40 minutes. All of a sudden, he hears the rumbling of thunder in the distance and notices that the sky is getting darker as large black clouds start showing over the trees that cover most of the Bender estate. It will be only a matter of minutes before a storm hits them. Garrett decides to use this change of weather and move up part of his plan. He calls Mo over to discuss this new thought.

Inside the house, Wayne hears the thunder. He can see it's getting darker outside. All of a sudden, he sees the digital clock on Scott's desk go out. He gets up from the desk and tries the light switch; the lights don't come on. Wayne knows whatever is going to happen is going to happen soon. A louder rumble of thunder shoots across the Bender home as the surrounding area quickly starts getting darker. Within a few minutes it's as dark as night and Wayne hears the first tapping of rain on the roof and windows. He leans back against the wall closest to the front foyer of Scott's office, and listens. The thunder outside progressively gets louder as the storm closes in around the Bender estate. The rain starts to come down a little harder as thunder sends another shock wave through the house, causing any loose items to shake and rattle.

Wayne isn't sure, but it sounded like one of the items rattling was a little too delayed. He crouches down and peers around the corner of the wall that leads into the front foyer. He is unable to make anything out at first so he slides across the floor in front of the steps leading upstairs. A flash of lightning and another crash of thunder rip through the house. Wayne tries to take advantage of the short burst of light from the lightning, but is unable to see anything out of the ordinary during the quick moment of light he had. It takes a few seconds for his eyes to readjust to the darkness, then decides to go back into Bender's office. He's at a disadvantage where he is now if anyone were to burst in from the front door since only a charred mattress stands between him and the outside. He stands up but stays low as he heads back to Scott's office. Another flash of light hits through the windows of the house as Wayne finishes his turn. In that exact second, Wayne catches a partial glimpse of someone standing next to him.

Wayne never sees the butt of the handgun that comes across his face; only his reflexes keep it from making a direct hit. It has enough force, though, to knock Wayne back a few feet, causing him to lose his balance. Reaching out, he grabs the end of the handrail of the stairs, but the attacker follows as Wayne reels backward. The attacker hits him square in the chest with a right leg sidekick. Wayne's body goes airborne a few feet, then hits the ground hard as his gun leaves his hand and slides across the floor.

Wayne recovers quickly and rolls to his left toward the back of the living room, but the attacker is on him with a front kick to Wayne's ribs. Wayne partially blocks the kick with his right forearm, but he still can feel the wind rushing out of his lungs from the force of the blow. The power of the kick, plus his own rolling momentum, continues his roll toward the back portion of the living room.

Another flash of lightning shoots through the windows of the living room just as the attacker readies another kick to Wayne's ribs. Wayne, seeing it coming out of the corner of his eye, performs a scissor kick to the attacker's weight bearing leg. The attacker grunts as he is flipped onto his back and crashes on the floor next to Wayne. Wayne follows this with a reverse heel kick to the attacker's chest. A forced exhale of air rushes from the attacker's body. While the attacker cringes in pain, Wayne kicks the gun from his hand and twirls to a crouched position in one motion. The attacker shakes off his pain and does a back thrust into a standing position as both face each other. With thunder rolling through the house, both wait to see what the other will do. The light from a bolt of lightning illuminates the room long enough for Wayne to make out the face of the attacker.

Wayne is stunned, for a brief period, by what he sees. The person standing across from him is supposed to be dead. Thunder from the most recent lightning sweeps the room. The rain from the storm is almost deafening as it slams against the windows and sides of the house from the increased wind.

"Mo?" Wayne asks with a hesitant tone.

"So you haven't forgotten your old buddy." Mo's tone is sarcastic, as Wayne and he were never buddies....

Back in their Marine days, Mo and Wayne had served in the same outfit. Mo was always a loner. He never really socialized with anyone as far as Wayne knew. While stationed together in Afghanistan after the attacks of 9-11, Wayne saw firsthand Mo's cruelty. During a routine patrol of a small village, their company came across a cache of guns and explosives hidden in a small hut outside of the main village. Wayne, a lieutenant at the time, was the one who discovered it and reported the find to his Captain, Mo Mower. Mo ordered the whole village rounded up and brought in for questioning. They held the interrogations in the small hut. Initially, three members of the unit went through the process of questioning villagers one by one. This went on without incident, but after about twenty villagers gave no answers as to how the weapons and explosives came to be in their village, Mo decided to take over the interrogations personally and privately.

Wayne challenged Mo's thinking since it went against the policies set up regarding interrogating civilians. Being alone while interrogating someone, especially a civilian, left the military open to many claims of abuse. Having other personnel involved, though not perfect, helped defend the actions taken. Mo ignored the advice and ordered Wayne to pull the troops back into the village along with the remaining civilians. He then proceeded to have his first civilian brought to him. Wayne didn't like this, but he followed his orders and moved everyone back into the village.

Twenty minutes later Mo walked back into the village. As he approached, Wayne could see him smiling.

"I have all the information we need, Lieutenant," Mo said with a tone of disdain toward Wayne. "Get the troops together and move out."

As Mo drew closer, Wayne could see fresh blood splattered on his clothing and face. Mo continued to walk past Wayne and headed into the village where the troops were waiting for him. Wayne turned away from Mo and looked in the direction of the small hut that Mo had just come from. Hesitating for only a second, he began to jog toward the hut. Mo looked back at Wayne, sensing he was not walking with him.

"Lieutenant," Mo yelled out to Wayne, "I gave you an order. Come back here and get the troops ready to move out."

Wayne started running faster to the hut. A couple of seconds later he reached the front door and pushed it open. To his horror, he saw the slight framed man the Captain questioned slumped in a chair, bleeding profusely from his face. Wayne rushed to him and grabbed his wrist to check for a pulse. He could barely feel one.

At that moment, Mo burst through the door, grabbed Wayne by the right arm, and pulled him away from the injured man in the chair.

"I gave you an order, Lieutenant," Mo angrily addressed Wayne. "Are you going to follow it, or do I put you on report?"

"This man is near death," Wayne firmly responded. "He needs

medical attention."

"The village people will take care of that, Lieutenant. I ordered you to move out."

Wayne looked outside as if to follow the orders given, then turned back to the injured man. Mo reacted furiously to this insubordination and reached for his sidearm. In one motion, the gun left its holster and slammed into the back of Wayne's head. Wayne collapsed to the ground, still conscious, but everything was fuzzy as he lay at Mo's feet. He heard Mo yell to the sergeant to get over here and put Lieutenant Mitchell under arrest for insubordination. Once the sergeant arrived and saw what was required, he called for a couple of troops to come in to the hut and help him carry Lieutenant Mitchell. The sergeant and two troopers grabbed Lieutenant Mitchell and took him, but not before they noticed the man bent over in the chair bleeding.

Wayne was never charged. Mower knew if he had pressed it, then what he did would be part of the investigation. Once Wayne recovered from the head wound, Mo ordered him to return to his position. Nobody referred to what happened during the remainder of the maneuvers. Soon after returning to base, Wayne requested a transfer, which Captain Mower quickly signed. Wayne finished his tour of duty with another regiment and never saw Captain Mower again.

Wayne became highly decorated during his remaining years in the Marines and was promoted to Captain before leaving to join the Secret Service. While an agent with the Secret Service, Wayne heard that Captain Mo Mower had also left the Marines and had become "a soldier of fortune" or a mercenary. Wayne knew that was what Mo should always have been; someone paid to fight for an army other than that of his country. Sometime after that, he heard Mo had been killed in Iraq trying to loot some of the country's treasures from its museums....

Now Mo is st..ring Wayne in the face, alive and as menacing as ever.

"I see you still like to hit people from behind," Wayne reminds Mo, remembering what Mo had done to him in Afghanistan.

"I had hoped you would appreciate a reliving of our history." Mo smiles with contempt.

"So our brief reunion will end here." Wayne acknowledges the obvious.

"Not necessarily. All you have to do is let me go through Bender's things to find what I'm here for. Once I find it, my men and I will be gone."

"Yeah," Wayne scoffs. "Even if I believed you, I can't let you do that."

"Wayne," Mo begins, "you tried to protect the villagers in Afghanistan and you couldn't. The same thing will happen to the women here if you try to stop me."

"There's one big difference," Wayne points out. "I don't have my back to you."

Seven

The Next Move

The rain continues to pound against the house as Wayne and Mo watch each other intently. Neither is sure what the next move should be. Wayne tries to look for either gun with his peripheral vision, but the near darkness in the room makes it impossible. He knows Mo is doing the same thing. Both know that the first move by either one will start the fight. Wayne can feel the knives he has in his belt, but he doesn't make a move to grab one yet. At that exact moment, a huge flash of lightning envelops the room followed by a crash of thunder. Both Wayne and Mo react instinctively and rush each other, Wayne going low while Mo attacks high.

In the split second it takes to reach each other, both have grabbed their knives and lashed at vital attack points of their opponent's body. Wayne, going low, thrusts his knife at one of the main arteries of Mo's left leg in hopes of providing an injury that will not kill and allow him to still talk. Mo, however, attacks high in hopes of dealing a fatal cut to Wayne's throat. As skilled as both are at dealing the wounds they attempted, they are also deft at avoiding such wounds. Realizing neither had hit their marks, they ready themselves for the next attempt.

Close knife fighting is a combination of skillful tactics and uncanny reflexes. Lacking either one will cause a quick end to your life. Mo attacks again the moment his feet hit the ground after his first lunge at Wayne. Wayne, already with both feet on the ground, rises to three quarters of his height and counters Mo's next assault. The knives move so quickly from thrust to parry, the low amount of light available barely allow them to see what the other is doing. Just pure instinct keeps them both alive.

The exchange of attacks has only lasted a few seconds when Wayne feels his first cut across his upper chest. The wound is not deep, but it's enough to tell him he isn't able to match Mo in this type of fight much longer. A second later Wayne feels a much deeper cut along his left forearm. Wayne twirls away from the exchange and squats to the ground. In the same instant, he plants his left foot and sidekicks into the darkness, hoping to hit his mark. He feels his foot hit Mo in the midsection, lifting him off the ground to crash against the wall that supports the staircase. Mo then bounces away from the wall and falls to the floor. Wayne, gets up, feels his way toward the back of the same wall, and ducks around the corner to the kitchen.

Wayne checks his wounds. None hit a vital artery, but he is bleeding and knows the cuts will need tending soon. Wayne knows how lucky he is this time. Another second or two and Mo would have probably killed him. He hears Mo getting up in the living room.

"What's wrong, Wayne?" Mo yells out. "Can't handle a little hand-to-hand combat anymore? The Secret Service sure has made you into a pussy. I remember a day when I would have thought twice before going against you, but all I see now is a coward who has run and hid. You might as well just kill those women and save me the trouble for all you can do for them."

Wayne knows he has lost a little pride, but he'll never let someone like Mo rile him enough with words into doing something stupid. Wayne will wait for the right time to challenge Mo again.

Mo waits for a few moments to see if he gets a rise out of Wayne, then realizes that's not going to happen. He's lost the advantage he once had.

Wayne knows the house and can use it in his favor. He's also probably gathering more weapons—something Mo is now lacking.

Mo quickly looks around the room for the handguns strewn about, but with the near dark conditions, cannot see them and doesn't want to have his back turned to Wayne while he looks. The rain continues to pummel the house as Mo reluctantly makes his way quietly out of the house.

Wayne crouches low and prepares for Mo's next attack. He listens intently, but all he can hear is the rain hammer against the house. Another burst of lightning and rippling thunder flows across the Bender estate. Wayne waits for only a few more seconds and decides to try to get back into the living room through Scott's office. Following the walls that connect the kitchen to Bender's office, Wayne slowly enters. With what little light there is, Wayne cannot see Mo. He continues cautiously toward the front of the office until he is again leaning against the wall that leads to the foyer. Wayne slowly peeks around the wall in time to see Mo already outside. Seconds later, he is out of sight.

Relieved he's not in the middle of a knife fight again, he goes into the living room and is able to locate both guns with the help of some timely lightning flashes. Heading upstairs, he calls out to the women to open the attic door. With the anxiousness of seeing a long-lost loved one, they tightly hug Wayne once he is inside. The hug lasts awhile as both women are afraid to let him go, but Kathy feels something wet seeping through her clothes.

"Oh my—" Kathy pushes back away from Wayne to get a better look—"you are hurt. Taylor, go down to my bathroom and get the first aid kit and bring it up here."

Wayne reaches out to Taylor to stop her. "No, it's too dangerous, I'll go."

He makes his way back down the attic stairs and is back in a minute. Kathy takes the kit from him and starts to dress Wayne's wounds. Luckily, he hasn't lost a lot of blood yet, but Kathy tells him that stitches will be required on the forearm cut. Until then Kathy wraps the wound tightly with gauze bandage after treating it and the chest cut with disinfectant. Wayne inspects the dressings and knows he couldn't have had better care by a medic on any battlefield.

"Thanks, Kathy."

Kathy smiles as they look at each other briefly. "Taylor and I were wondering if," Kathy hesitates, "we could use the washroom?"

Wayne smiles.

"And any chance we can get some food from the kitchen?" Taylor adds.

Again, Wayne smiles. "I'll see if I can get something from the refrigerator."

Wayne heads down the attic stairs first. A few minutes later they are all back in the attic, a little more refreshed and eager to eat what Wayne had brought from the kitchen. Wayne knows he can only spend a little time with them before he has to get back downstairs. He watches them eat the lunchmeats and fruit he brought and wishes he could feel better about their safety.

He also brought a jug of water from their purified bottle water supply to keep them hydrated, as the attic is quite warm. The dark skies and rain have allowed the attic to stay cooler than normal, but it's still warm. Wayne looks at his watch—almost 3:30 p.m. Time to get back downstairs. He tells Kathy and Taylor to keep the baseball bats close, then closes the attic door behind him.

Outside, Mo stands in a makeshift tent out of the pounding rain.

"You had him, yet you tell me he's still alive," Garrett Coffman responds angrily to Mo's take on what happened. "When did you become so incompetent?"

Of course, Mo now realizes he shouldn't have given Wayne the professional courtesy of not shooting him in the back, but he so wanted to see the look on his face.

Garrett gestures past Mo to the group of men walking toward them through the rain. "Well, it's good I don't have to rely on you to get what I need." Garrett shoots a scathing look back at Mo. "Go watch the house and see if you can at least keep them inside. We're now going straight at them."

Mo turns angrily away from Garrett and back into the rain.

A few seconds later, the other men are in the tent with Garrett. Mo watches from the side of the house, paying more attention to the activity in the tent than what might be happening in or around the house. Garrett has never dismissed him before and Mo will make sure it never happens again.

Back in the house, Wayne knows he has few options left...and little hope. He isn't sure how many men are still out there and knows it will be hours before anyone will be concerned that he hasn't checked in. They've tried a two-front attack and sent in a hand-to-hand combat specialist. Even though time isn't on Wayne's side, it's also not on theirs. Wayne worries they won't waste any more time and will just rush the house commando style—in full force, pouring through the doorways and windows, hoping to overwhelm him.

Eight

In Full Force

A s Wayne sets up his last line of defense, thunder continues to rumble around the house. The rain is a persistent deafening noise against the outside walls, making it impossible to hear anything coming from outside. An occasional lightning strike illuminates the house and yard briefly, but not enough to give Wayne any real feel for what is happening outside.

He readjusts the remaining two knives in his belt and checks Scott's handgun to make sure it is loaded and ready. He checks Mo's gun, a Berretta 92FS, and finds it has a full clip of 15 rounds in it of 9mm shells. This gun, designated with the name M9 by the U.S. Military, always exceeded testing requirements. Wayne may be out-manned, but he isn't outgunned with Scott's snub-nose and now the Berretta. He'll have twenty shots before he'll have to reload.

He decides that the best location to fend off any attack is from the living room. From there, with the fireplace to his back, he can defend against anyone coming into the main part of the house and pick anyone off trying to get upstairs. Wayne quickly gathers the furniture from the room and positions it around the fireplace. He then sits behind the crude barricade and waits. The wind is picking up and now howling as it hurls the rain even harder against the house. The gusts have to be close to 30 miles an hour as Wayne can see one of the smaller trees in the front yard whipping back and forth.

Even with all the noise from the storm, Wayne hears a clang of metal against the house. At first, he tries to convince himself that it is something the wind threw, but he realizes he cannot take the risk. Slowly he gets out from behind the furniture and walks from window to window trying to see out. There just is not sufficient angle available from his position to see enough to satisfy him. He hurriedly considers trying to sneak outside when he hears another sound—one that sends a shock through his heart.

"Oh no, they're on the roof!" Wayne exclaims as he races to the stairs.

Taking the stairs three steps at a time, he is at the top in the exact moment the windows from the master bedroom and Kathy's office come crashing in, followed by a wave of thunder and a flash of lightning. Wayne, seeing only shadows and brief glimpses of the intruders, goes into a forward roll and dives into the laundry room on his left. Lying flat on the floor, Wayne waits for his opportunities.

The first dark image Wayne sees comes through Kathy's office door; a second later, the intruder is repelled back into the office with a shot to his chest from one of Wayne's guns. Wayne, using the last bullet in his SIG Sauer P229, holsters it, then quickly grabs the Berretta and turns his attention to movement coming from the master bedroom. Short bursts from automatic weapons shred the doorframe to the laundry room as Wayne rolls to his left behind the wall. Shots now come from another person in Kathy's office, forcing Wayne to plaster himself against the wall to avoid the hail of bullets slamming into the other side. Wayne does his best to return fire, but with limited visibility and ammo, he knows he cannot do much except keep them away from the attic.

Wayne understands his desperate situation. Soon they will rush the room...overpower and kill him. He can only hope to take some down before that happens. He readies his guns and prepares for the next assault. All of a sudden, he hears a crash from downstairs followed by automatic gunfire as heavy footsteps run up the stairs. Shots then begin whizzing past the laundry door from the stairs, but instead of hitting anything near Wayne, they hit the master bedroom and Kathy's office. A bolt of lightning brings a familiar face into view.

As the gunfire mingles with the thunder, Wayne comes out of the laundry room in a crouched position firing toward Kathy's office while the man coming up the stairs continues his barrage on the master bedroom. The men in those rooms, surprised by the unexpected attack, retreat out the windows and out onto the roof. Wayne rushes into Kathy's office in time to send a couple of bullets into a man trying to reach the ladder. He collapses to the roof, then takes the 15-foot plunge to the ground. The others are out of sight, obviously taking another route down from the master bedroom.

Wayne turns from the window and walks back to the hallway where the last person he expected was standing. "Austin!"

The two men exchanged a brief hug.

"I can't believe it," Wayne said. "How did you…hey, I don't really care! I'm just glad you're here. How many agents are there?"

"The rest are taking the ones we caught in for questioning," Austin explains.

"One is Mo Mower," Wayne points out.

"Mo Mower?" Austin reacts in surprise, for he also knows of Mower through his relationship with Wayne.

"Yes, I know, but it's him," Wayne confirms.

"Well, we should have gotten all of them since there is only one way out of here," Austin reassures Wayne.

Wayne goes downstairs in time to see the remaining cars taking the path to the front gate as the heavy rain continues.

How quickly things can change, he realizes. *My prayers were certainly tested this time.* Another few minutes and Austin would have been too late.

Wayne takes Austin up into the attic and introduces him to the Benders, then explains their friendship. Austin is a couple inches shorter than Wayne and a couple of years older, but his face has boyish features that make him look younger, like his mid-length blond hair and great physical shape.

"Look—" Austin interrupts all the pleasantries—"some more agents are on their way to escort the Benders to a safe location, so we'll need to hole up in the house until they arrive. With all the disagreeable things down on the lower floors, it might be best to just wait up here."

Wayne appreciates Austin's concern for what might be very upsetting for the women to see, with all the bodies and destruction about the house. He agrees with him and confirms that it's best to wait here for the other agents. They all find a comfortable place to sit.

"Mr. Ivers," Kathy begins.

"Please, call me Austin, Mrs. Bender."

Kathy smiles and continues, "And you must call me Kathy. Would you like something to eat? We have a variety of lunchmeats and fruit."

"No, thank you, Kathy. I already had something to eat."

Kathy smiles again. "Taylor and I tried to eat earlier, but with everything that has happened, I must admit the food didn't have any real taste. Now, though, I have a feeling it will taste a lot better." Kathy reaches for some lunchmeat and fruit and offers it to Taylor and Wayne, who take a little of both.

Wayne leans back in his makeshift chair of cushions with his fruit and lunchmeats.

"So ladies," Austin says, "I know this couldn't have been how you envisioned this day."

Kathy and Taylor chuckled lightly.

"I do want to say how sorry I am for your loss. I know it cannot be easy for you," Austin said.

"Thank you. Even without all that has happened today, this has been very tough for us," Kathy replied. "I just wish I knew what those men were after. Wayne thought it might be the same thing he came for."

Kathy offering that information to Austin catches Wayne off guard. "Yes, I'm afraid it is," he admitted, "and it's nowhere in Scott's desk." Wayne adds that last bit in an attempt to end that part of the conversation.

"Do you know what it is that makes it so important, Wayne?" Kathy prods.

Knowing he cannot discuss the item, he replies, "Just as I said earlier, it has national security concerns."

Kathy shakes her head, as if knowing Wayne isn't telling all he knows.

A few moments of silence take over the attic before Austin speaks.

"So neither you nor Taylor knows about this item?"

Both women look at each other and shrug.

"Man—" Austin looks at the floor—"it's sad you two will probably have to be in protective custody indefinitely, because it doesn't look like whoever is trying to get this item will stop coming after you until they do."

"That's enough, Austin," Wayne says firmly.

Austin frowns. "I'm just trying to point out that if they know of it, they need to produce it so they can get on with their lives. Or at least inform you of other possible places it could be."

Wayne reluctantly has to acknowledge Austin's point. "Kathy, Agent Ivers is right. Until, at some point, it's believed you are safe, you and Taylor will have to remain under guard."

"You mean this isn't over?" Kathy responds in disbelief.

"Probably not," Wayne replies.

"Could Scott have hid it someplace that isn't normally used?" Austin asks with a somewhat impatient voice.

Wayne turns to him with a cold stare. "That's enough, Austin. We'll talk about it when we get back to Washington." He then turns back to Kathy. "I'm sorry, he means…"

But Wayne is unable to finish his sentence because a cold piece of metal presses against the back of his head, followed by the click of a gun cocking.

"No, Wayne," Austin corrects him, "we will talk about it now."

Nine

Something Was Wrong

Kathy and Taylor both are jolted back on their cushions in shock.

"But you are friends," Taylor says, her voice alarmed.

"We *were* friends," Wayne corrects Taylor. "I just didn't want to believe something was wrong with this rescue. Even when you told Kathy you had already eaten, since we were to meet for dinner at 5 and it is now just," Wayne lifts his watch arm, "4:53."

Wayne hears Austin chuckle behind him. "Just as I was saying that, I knew I may have let something slip. I was hoping you'd be glad enough that I was here to let a few inconsistencies slide. When they called me to say you were with the Benders, I knew our days of friendship were over. Too bad you cancelled our golf. I'd much rather beat you on the course than do it here. If we could have been sure Bender hadn't left the journal here, all this could have been avoided, but conversations were overheard that led us to believe it is here."

"So they send you," Wayne says sarcastically.

Austin hesitates. "We tried coming in through the front door. I don't know if that would have worked, but it quickly became apparent that with you here, the easy way was not going to happen and any more direct assaults could leave all of you dead before we could ask any questions about the ledger's location. Obviously, Wayne, we hoped to get its location by using our friendship and the fact that it looked like I had just saved all of your lives."

Then Austin leans close to Wayne's ear so only Wayne can hear. "As you seem to know, Bender and the President have been compiling this list for years. Bender acknowledged its existence when he threatened the release of certain parts to stop a popular political figure from opposing the President's agenda. Having a list is one thing; using it to threaten good people because things aren't going your way, well, we had to stop it."

A chill races through Wayne. *Is Austin saying Bender's death wasn't an accident and that he's part of it? Are other agents involved?*

"Now," Austin directs his conversation to Kathy and Taylor, "let's get down to business. Ladies, unless I get some help here soon, I'm going to have to hurt our friend Wayne."

Austin changes the direction of the gun from pointing to Wayne's head to his knee. "I'll use the old standby of giving you till the count of three, if that will help. One..." He waits a couple of seconds. "Two..."

Taylor yells out, "No!"

Austin smiles. "You have something to say?"

"No, she doesn't," Wayne interrupts.

"She is trying to save you a lot of pain, so you might want to let her talk," Austin retorts.

"Taylor," Wayne turns to her to explain, "you don't have to tell him anything, because he won't shoot me."

Austin smiles. "Well, I guess I'll just have to show them." Austin trains the gun barrel at Wayne's leg.

Taylor and Kathy both yell out, "No!"

A second later Austin's Secret Service issued SIG Sauer P229 hammer releases. Both women flinch in anticipation of the expected blast of gunfire, but nothing but the click of metal hitting metal is heard. A second passes and a couple of more clicks sound as Wayne slowly turns toward Austin while drawing the SIG Sauer P229 he still had in his holster. He then points it at Austin.

"You see, Austin," Wayne begins, "I may not have wanted to believe something was wrong, but, like you said, a few inconsistencies were quick to come to mind. Not wanting to take any chances, when we hugged, I took the opportunity to switch my gun, which I knew was empty, with yours."

Austin drops the empty gun and shakes his head in frustration.

"There is no way you could have known where I was since the President himself asked me to do this secretly," Wayne explained. "Moreover, there hadn't been enough time for him to be alarmed to call in help. Considering what he sent me for, he would have waited until the last possible moment to send in reinforcements. If any civilian had called, concerned they couldn't get through to the Benders, they would have called the police, not the Secret Service. There were just too many reasons you should not be here."

Austin gave a weak smile at Wayne's logic.

"I didn't want to completely rule out dumb luck, though," Wayne continues, "so I didn't question you on how you got here. I was afraid you would give an obviously weak explanation which would have kept us from getting where we are now, with you explaining why everyone is here and me holding the loaded gun."

"You won't be going anywhere," Austin states. "Those cars you saw leaving were just going to the gate to wait for me to come out. As soon as they see you try to leave, they'll be all over you."

Wayne figured as much. "Kathy, I hate to ask you, but I left a roll of duct tape on Scott's desk. Would you get it and bring it back? I'd go myself, but I'm afraid our friend here would test your resolve to fire a gun at him, and I don't want to put you in that position."

Kathy begins to walk to the attic door.

"Take this gun." Wayne hands her the Berretta. "There shouldn't be anyone downstairs, but take it just in case."

Kathy reaches for the gun and takes it from Wayne's hand.

"There will be some disturbing sights. Do your best to ignore them and come back quickly."

Kathy descends the attic stairs and sees the destruction of her beautiful home. It is still dark from the storm outside but as she gets down the attic stairs, the bullet-riddled doorframe to the laundry room comes into sight. As she walks down to the first floor, a strong odor she isn't familiar with permeates the air. Soon what is causing the stench comes into view, and she covers her mouth in horror.

A person, horribly burned, is hanging from a rake near what used to be the front door. Kathy, as fast as she can, reaches the bottom of the stairs and turns into Scott's office. The duct tape is lying on Scott's desk; she quickly grabs it and hurries back to the attic. Kathy calls out to Wayne, and a second later Taylor opens the door so Kathy can come up.

While Kathy is gone, Wayne has Taylor look for an old pillowcase to put over Austin's head. With the darkness from the storm, he feels he can pull off his plan. Kathy finishes climbing the steps into the attic and hands Wayne the duct tape. It only takes a minute to tape Austin's hands behind his back and put a piece over his mouth. Wayne then has him stand and walk to the attic door.

"I can't get down those stairs like this," Austin declares.

"Well, I guess I can push you down the stairs," Wayne replies curtly.

Under the pillowcase, Austin's face shows his resignation to having to feel his way down the stairs. Wayne goes first without disclosing it to Austin, wanting to keep him unsure of where Wayne is from now on. Austin feels, with his feet, where the steps are and slowly navigates his way down to the second floor laundry room. Once everyone is down from the attic, Wayne turns to the women.

"When we leave and are away from the house, those people outside will come in and scour this house for Scott's ledger. Before we leave, I need to ask if it could be somewhere in the house?"

The women look at each other. Kathy is the first to speak. "I cannot think of anywhere else it could be. We don't have a bank lock box that I know of. When Scott died, both of us went through his things and I checked our wall safe to get our copy of his will and other legal documents. I found nothing that resembles what you are describing. Taylor, you went through his desk. Did you find anything like a ledger?"

Taylor turns to Wayne angrily. "Wayne, if you didn't find it, it's not there."

Realizing he has just questioned their integrity, Wayne accepts their answers and leads the way down the stairs to the first floor. Kathy tells Taylor to not look around and hold her breath until they get outside. Kathy then holds Taylor's hand and helps her down the stairs, past the burned person hanging from the rake.

At the home's front door, Wayne pulls off the pillowcase, pushes Austin in front, and tells the women to walk in front on either side of him. This will give anyone watching the perception that Austin is leading everyone out to Wayne's car, maybe to take him to the location of the journal. For that reason, it won't seem odd for Wayne to drive. With the women close to Austin's sides, Wayne is hoping that the heavy rain and darkness from the storm will keep those watching from noticing Austin's hands taped behind him and the tape on his mouth. It's a risk Wayne feels he has to take. The people watching will then contact those at the front gate, hopefully to let them pass.

Upon reaching Wayne's car, Wayne has Kathy sit in the back seat with Austin while he and Taylor take the front seat. Inside the car, Wayne tells Kathy to keep the Berretta trained on Austin, but out of sight. As they drive to the gate, Austin's situation should not be apparent through the tinted windows of the Secret Service issued car. If they get past the gate, Wayne will have to bide his time on when to lose the cars, which will undoubtedly follow just out of sight.

Ten

Everything Seemed Calm

"**S**ir, we have a radio call from one of the men watching the house. He says they are coming out."

Garrett Coffman grabs the radio handset from the man. "All of them?"

"Yes, sir," comes the reply from the other end. "They are getting into one of the cars and look to be leaving."

"Was Austin in trouble?" Garrett asks.

"It didn't look like it, sir. They said it was hard to make out anything specific, but the women were next to him and everything seemed calm."

Garrett gives back the handset to the other man and stares out into the woods for a few seconds to collect his thoughts. "Tell that guy to stay out of sight," he barks.

The man with the radio relays the order as Garrett turns to Mo standing near the entrance gate to the Bender estate: "Get your men back into the trees and out of sight and pull the cars down the street, but I want you in a car to follow the car coming out. Be sure to radio in to me where they go."

Mo acknowledges the order and goes about to follow it as Garrett turns back to the man holding the radio set. "I will assume Austin has gotten their confidence and is going with them, hopefully, to get the journal." Garrett pauses. "But there is another possibility. He could have been overpowered, is just a prisoner, and now they're leaving with the journal. That's where Mo will come in."

The man holding the radio is listening.

"When the car is past us and through the gate," Garrett continues, "go into the house and search it thoroughly. Maybe Austin is just getting them out of the house for us."

The other man nods in agreement as they both duck behind some trees. Soon the lights from Wayne's car show through the trees, heading toward the entrance gate of the estate. The car approaches at a conservative speed that does not cause any concern from those watching behind the trees. The car hesitates near the gate entrance so the sensor can open it. The gate slowly opens as Garrett tries to look into the vehicle, but the tinted windows, the darkness, and rain keep him from seeing anything. The car pulls slowly through the gate and turns right onto the road in front of the gate. Moments later, the car is out of sight, but with a black car following a hundred yards behind.

Garrett watches Wayne's car go out of sight, then motions for his men to head to the Bender house to give it a complete going over. If the ledger is in the house, they will find it. As the men search through the house, the rain starts to turn more to a sprinkle and the skies begin to lighten. A couple of men retrieve the bodies of their dead, along with the CJ9As placed around the house to block the cell phone calls.

On a road, about five miles from the Bender estate, Wayne Mitchell is trying to decide what he's going to do about the car following behind by about a hundred yards. He tests his cell phone and sees he now has reception. For a quick second he thinks about calling for help from the Secret Service office, but reconsiders after remembering what Austin said about "we had to stop it" and his fear that maybe other agents are involved. He knows that he has to get the women to safety, but what will the car following do if he heads to the White House?

He approaches the entrance to Highway 50/301 and takes the entrance ramp going west toward Washington. Once on the highway he begins to pick up speed.

Back in the following black car, Mo reaches for his cell phone and makes a call.

A few seconds later Garrett Coffman answers, "Yes."

"They have turned onto 50/301 going west at a high rate of speed. They could be making a run for it."

There is a pause before Garrett responds, "I'm sure Austin has not said anything yet, but we can't take any chances in case he is not in control. Follow for a while longer, but if they don't get off before Bowie, you'll have to take care of Austin. Try to get the rest, but Austin has to be eliminated. He can tie too many things together."

Mo tells Garrett he understands and hangs up the cell phone. Mo has never really liked Austin, so killing him is not a problem. As they pull onto 50/301 west, it's quickly apparent something is wrong. Mitchell's car is substantially farther ahead and traveling even faster. Mo tells his driver to "floor it" and gets his rifle case from the back seat. He methodically opens the case and attaches the scope to his USMC M40A3.

The design of this rifle makes it extremely accurate and a superb sniper rifle. Combined with the new M118LR ammo (or in sniper parlance AA11) makes it ranked with the best in the world. It has a range of 1000 yards and is capable of surgical precision shooting. A trained sharpshooter, Mo started his tour with the Marines as a sniper and some of his targets were moving at high rates of speed, so he feels very confident as he instructs the driver to get at least within 200 yards before Mitchell's car can get off the Chesapeake Bay Bridge. From that distance, the rounds should easily find their marks. As Mo's car approaches the Chesapeake Bay Bridge, he props the barrel of the rifle on the piece of metal attaching the side view mirror to the car. It proves to be an acceptable mount as he leans out the window and checks his sight alignment.

There aren't as many cars on the Chesapeake Bay Bridge going toward Washington as there are leaving as it is now almost 6 p.m. and most are on their way home away from Washington. Mo's driver swerves into the left lane of the two lanes going west as he continues to avoid cars to get closer to Mitchell's car. It doesn't take long before the cars are within 200 yards of each other. Mo centers his sight on the back of Austin's head, which is easy to make out through the powerful scope as he sits in the back right seat of Mitchell's car.

Wayne has been unable to pick up a visual of the black car that had been following until it suddenly swerves into the left lane. The car is well back but closing quickly. Just as Wayne is about to depress the accelerator more, an explosion of glass engulfs the car's interior. In a fraction of a second both the back window and right front side window shatter into a million pieces. Wayne, shocked by the unexpected mayhem, jerks the car to the left into the path of oncoming traffic. Amid the shriek of horns from the approaching vehicles, he brings the car under control and back into the westward flow of traffic.

Blood splatters the windshield and dashboard. "Is anyone hurt?" Wayne yells out as he tries to keep his eyes trained on the road.

"I'm okay except for some small glass cuts," Taylor calls out.

"I'm all right," Kathy calls from the back seat, "but I think Austin is hurt."

Kathy leans over to check on Austin, now slumped forward and leaning against the right back door. Just as she does, another shot passes over her head and shatters the front windshield. Wayne shoves the gas-peddle to the floor.

"Get down!" Wayne yells.

Within a couple of seconds, they are traveling at over 90 miles an hour and weaving in and out of cars. Occasionally he looks into the rearview mirror, but his quick glimpses are unable to see anyone following at first. A few seconds later, he notices a black car veering back and forth, passing vehicles at a rapid pace. Wayne knows he has to get off this bridge fast. The first exit he can take, Oceanic Drive, is coming up on the right. He swerves back into the right lane just before the exit and turns onto the exit ramp at nearly 80 miles an hour, slowing down just enough not to flip the car off the ramp.

Wayne knows this road will take him to Sandy Point State Park where there are park police. Without knowing if there are other agents involved, Wayne feels this will be a good way to protect the Bender women. In seconds he is at the entrance to the park where a short line to get in has formed. Wayne checks his rearview mirror, but isn't able to see the black car as a small pickup truck pulls behind him to get into the park. He knows he didn't lose them, but with so many cars and people around, they may be staying back to see what happens.

A minute later Wayne pulls up to the entrance and shows the attendant his credentials while telling him to get the park police and an ambulance. He then pulls his car behind the entrance building to wait for the police. Wayne turns around and leans over the seat to look at Austin, who is still slumped forward against the back right door. He immediately sees it wasn't necessary to have them call an ambulance. Austin is bleeding heavily from a large entrance wound to the back of his head. Knowing the bullet passed through Austin and into the front side window, Wayne doesn't lift Austin up, not wanting to show the women a large facial wound.

Soon a couple of park police cars pull up to Wayne's car. Within seconds four policemen are helping take Wayne and the two women to a safe location while a park ranger stays with Austin's body until the ambulance arrives. Wayne immediately tells the officers not to contact anyone outside the park. That it has to remain a Secret Service matter because of its national security issues.

The police take the three to the park headquarters. Once Wayne has secured the protection of the women, he asks to borrow a car.

Before leaving, Wayne goes to the women, who are now safe in a secure room in the park police headquarters. "I have to leave, but you are both safe here. The officers will be with you until I can come back. They have promised to have someone with you continually. They are going to make up some sleeping accommodations, and you'll have all the food and drink you need. Don't answer your cell phones. Keep them turned off. Whoever did this can track you by homing in on the signal if you answer them. The officers have my cell number and will call me from their land line if they need to."

"Where are you going?" Taylor asks, frightened.

"There has been a security breach. I have to try to find out what's happened and stop any further damage. I'll come back for you both as quick as possible."

Wayne gives some final instructions to the park police, then leaves the headquarters to get the car they have given him. He hates to go, but he knows leaving the women with the park police is the best option he had. Taking them with him would put their lives in further danger, since he isn't sure what will be waiting for him outside of the park. Hoping to leave the park unobserved, Wayne takes one of the service roads the police tell him to use.

Eleven

Make New Plans

Mo decides not to pursue Wayne off the highway once he sees where he's going. Instead, he tells his driver to return to the office. He then places a call back to Garrett to give him an update and to tell him to leave the Bender estate as quickly as possible, for it could be swarming with federal agents soon.

Garrett acknowledges the need to wrap things up and tells his men just that, but tells Mo to turn around and wait for reinforcements at the park entrance. Garrett has been unable to find the journal anywhere in the house. Something that important could only be one place else. He will have to make new plans. Once all the men are out of the house and the bodies are collected, they too head to the park.

Soon Wayne is back on highway 50/301 west; he looks in his rearview mirror, almost hoping to see the black car following him. That way he would at least know where it is. About 40 minutes later, he is pulling up to the entrance of the West Wing of the White House. Three minutes after that, he's sitting in the Oval Office, waiting for the President to arrive and trying to figure out how Austin got involved. Thinking back on what little Austin divulged, how would he have known Bender was using the list as a threat and who was the "we" he referred to when he said, "we had to stop it." *Was Bender's death planned?* Wayne asks himself.

Wayne hears the unmistakable commotion of an entourage of an approaching President outside the entrance door of the Oval Office. Seconds later the President comes through the door, leaving everyone else outside. Wayne is already standing to greet the President, but the President motions for Wayne to take a seat in one of the chairs in front of his desk as he sits next to him.

"Do you have it?" the President asks anxiously.

"No, Mr. President. It wasn't at the house, but we have an even bigger problem."

The President's expression changes from disappointment to startled.

"While I was there," Wayne continues, "we were attacked by a large, heavily armed, group."

"Attacked?" The President sits up in his chair. "Are Kathy and Taylor…?" He can't bring himself to finish the sentence.

"They are fine, Mr. President."

"Thank God." The President relaxes a bit in his chair.

"I'm not sure who was leading the attack, but they were after the list."

"But how would they have known about it?"

"Sir, were you aware that Scott had been using the list to quiet opposition to your legislative agenda and that he threatened to have certain parts published?" Wayne bluntly asks.

The President lowers his head into his hands, "Dear God, no," he whispers. A moment later the President lifts his head heavenward and asks, "How can this have happened?" Then he looks at Wayne. "He had come to me last year wanting to use it when another of my bills before Congress was heading for defeat. He pointed out that many opposing me were on the list. However, I told him that the list was not for that purpose. I reminded him it was only to keep track of who owed us favors or whom we owed favors too. It was never meant to be used to blackmail."

"Well, whoever sent that group to the house was going to make sure it was not ever going to be used that way," Wayne points out.

"What worries me the most is that they knew it wasn't in Bender's West Wing office."

"Yes, I see what you mean," the President says, following Wayne's train of thought.

"I'm afraid the leak may be coming from the Secret Service," Wayne adds.

The President shakes his head in disbelief. "How could that be? You people are screened more thoroughly than I was."

"One of the attackers was Agent Austin Ivers," Wayne explains.

The President gasps in shock. "President Osburn's lead agent while he was President?"

"Yes," Wayne answers bluntly.

"This is unbelievable. Do you know of any other agents?" the President asks.

"No, but I'd worry about the one you had look for the list in Scott's office."

"Oh no!" The President gasps again. His lead agent, Tim Peters. "Tim has been with me since I first ran for President. I know he was upset that I didn't confide in him when I took that trip with you last year. I was informed he was particularly disturbed that you had to then save my life because I went on that trip, but to act against the office of the President? Heck, his brother, Mike, is also a respected agent assigned to protect…"

"Until we can rule him out, you'll need to keep him on a short leash," Wayne explains.

The President nods heavily.

"For the time being, I'll need to work on this alone. I can't risk taking anyone else into our confidence yet. I left the Benders with the park police at Sandy Point State Park—the only law enforcement agency I'm sure is not a part of this. For the time being, don't send anyone to the Bender residence. It would just cause a lot of media attention and hinder my actions. Let them think they're still operating undetected. The funeral is not for a few days and the Benders had asked for that time to be alone anyway, so nothing will seem that unusual. If you could have your secretary contact the Benders' phone service provider to not allow any calls in as if requested by them, that should eliminate inquiries about their not answering calls."

"What will you be doing?"

"I'm going to push some people and see if I get a reaction." Wayne gets up from his chair and turns to leave. When he reaches the Oval Office door he turns back to the President, "In addition, Mr. President, I'd make sure you get a team you can trust at that crash site. There might be something of interest on the black box recording."

When Wayne opens the door to leave, his thoughts run wildly. He has some detective work ahead of him. He needs to find out if Scott Bender had a lockbox his wife is not aware of and if so, where? He starts walking down the corridor from the Oval Office to the corner office of the White House chief of staff. There the only person who would have that information sits in a small office just to the side of the chief of staff's office.

"Hello, Nancy," Wayne says to Bender's long-time secretary, Nancy Roberts. She stands next to her desk trying to organize the transfer of Benders' office to the next chief of staff when named.

Nancy looks up. Her eyes are red from hours of crying.

"Wayne, it's so good to see you." She barely gets the words out before she starts crying again. "They told me to take time off until after the funeral, but I just couldn't sit home. This way I know everything is being taken care of the way Mr. Bender would have wanted."

Wayne hates to have to ask her anything that might cause her to get upset again, but he has a limited amount of time. "Nancy, I hate to bother you now with this, but Kathy Bender needs to know if there's a lockbox you are aware of that Mr. Bender maintained."

Nancy knows that Wayne is a close confidant of the Benders. "Yes, of course she would need to know that." She searches through her desk a couple of seconds and hands Wayne a small red envelope. "Here's the key."

Wayne takes the small envelope from Nancy. It has a large side view of an eagle's head followed by the word *EagleBank* embossed on it. He opens the envelope and sees the lockbox key inside.

"Don't ask me why he picked that one," Nancy added. "I think he liked that it had a community bank atmosphere. The box is located at the DuPont Circle branch. I know that because I was with him once when he stopped there and he said he had to go in for a minute to put something in his box. He gave me the spare key in case he left his at home."

Wayne nodded. "Thank you, Nancy. I'll make sure Kathy gets it."

Wayne turns to leave, but Nancy stops him. "You have to sign for it." Nancy holds out a pen and a receipt pad.

"Of course." Wayne, a little embarrassed, reaches for the pen and pad and signs his name.

"Please date it too, Wayne."

Wayne adds the date to his signature, then again thanks Nancy before he leaves. As he makes his way out of the West Wing of the White House, he knows he'll have to go back to Sandy Point State Park and find a way to get Kathy and Taylor safely to the White House. Coming from the outside now, Wayne will be able to make sure no one is lurking outside of the park. He knows the White House is the best place for them until he repairs the security breach. In addition, DuPont Circle is only a few blocks from the White House, so he'll be able to get Kathy safely there and back.

Once outside the West Wing, he quickly strides to his car and heads out of the west security gate. Wayne looks at his watch: *8:11 p.m.* He knows the park is probably closed, but he was planning to use the back service road he had taken to leave so that shouldn't be a problem. Before going back into the park, he'll check its perimeter to make sure it's safe to bring them out. He should be there by about 9 p.m.

Twelve

No Signs

A little before 9 p.m. Wayne is pulling into the service road entrance of Sandy Point State Park. He has already driven the perimeter of the park and found nothing to cause him concern. The park doesn't use the road during off hours so Wayne doesn't expect any outgoing traffic. Being dark now, he takes the road somewhat slower than he did earlier since it's not paved, and there are many ruts in the road. A few minutes later, he pulls up to the lighted parking lot of the office that houses the police station headquarters.

The first thing Wayne notices is all the cars still there. The office personnel must work late. He gets out of the car and walks toward the front entrance. As he approaches, he notices a small hole with crack lines around it in the window just left of the front door. A bullet hole. He crouches down and draws his gun. He remembers the receptionist sat on the other side of that window.

Wayne moves quickly to the railing of the front porch, straining to hear any movement from inside the building. Hearing nothing after a few seconds, he slowly peers through the receptionist's window. There is no sign of anyone moving inside. Wayne reaches for the front door handle. It turns easily. He pushes and the door swings open. Wayne plasters himself against the front of the building next to the open door, waiting to see if there is any reaction from inside.

When there is no reaction from the door opening, Wayne slowly enters and visually takes in the area. As he passes through the entrance, he turns left, to the receptionist's counter, and looks over it. On the floor, with a single bullet to the head, lies the receptionist. Wayne goes around and takes her hand, since whether it is warm or not will give him a feel for how long she has been dead. The hand is still slightly warm. He gathers she's been dead for less than an hour.

Wayne continues his progress through the lower floor of the building. Just past the reception area, he sees the coffee room. Coffee is still on the burners, but no one is in the room. In the next room two people slump backwards at their workstations with single bullet wounds to the head. Across the hall is the police area, where Kathy and Taylor are supposed to be. He turns the door handle and pushes the door open while he stays back. There is no sound coming from this area either as his fears for Kathy and Taylor now overwhelm him.

Wayne composes himself and steps through the door. The first encounter is with a fallen officer, half propped up in the left corner of the office. Two wounds are clearly visible, one to the chest and one to the head. A second officer is just to the right. He is facedown in a sprawled position, blood covering the floor under him. The room he left Kathy and Taylor in is next to the second dead officer. The door to the room is half-open and seriously damaged, as if it were kicked open.

Inside that room another officer lies on his side in a pool of blood, but no one else is there. Wayne is relieved the women aren't dead, but scared too. Kathy and Taylor may be alive, but for how long? He hurriedly checks the rest of the building and surrounding area for any other bodies. Finding no one else, he heads out to his car. Wayne knows he has only one place to go to find some answers.

On his way to the White House, he calls the President and briefs him of his findings at the park. The President says he'll have someone brief the police before they go to the scene. Wayne then asks the President to tell Agent Tim Peters to go relax in the Secret Service office for the remainder of the evening before turning in. This isn't unusual since it's past 10 p.m. The Secret Service office is a large room directly below the cabinet room and the Oval Office, easy for an agent to get back quickly to the President if needed.

Wayne then calls Nancy Roberts' office. As he fears, she has left for the evening. He then calls the White House switchboard and asks them to transfer him to her home phone. A few rings later, Nancy's familiar voice answers. Wayne asks her if she had the cell phone numbers of Kathy and Taylor. She tells him they would be in her office in her rolodex on her desk. He thanks her and hangs up.

About 40 minutes later he's back at the White House and entering the ground floor of the West Wing. He heads first for Nancy's office to locate the cell phone numbers. He then calls a friend in the FBI and asks him to place a trace on those numbers and to call him if there is any activity. He explains the late night need as a possible threat to the President.

When Wayne finally enters the Secret Service room, Agent Tim Peters is sitting in front of the television, drinking some coffee. Only a few agents usually occupy the Secret Service office at a time unless there is a special event going on. Late at night, there is sometimes none. Tonight there is only Peters and Mitchell.

As Wayne steps farther into the room, Tim looks up from his coffee and turns to see who is there. Agent Peters is a ruggedly handsome man standing 6 feet 6 inches with medium complexion and dark hair. Like Wayne, he came from the military ranks and held the military heavy weight boxing title until he left to become a Secret Service Agent. A few years later he helped get his younger brother, Mike, into the Secret Service.

"What brings you here?" Tim asks.

Wayne smiles, remembering what the President had said earlier in the day about Tim being upset that the President asked Wayne to accompany him on that fateful trip last year. As the President stated, Tim was assigned to protect him once he became an official candidate for the Presidency and has been with him ever since. To be out of the loop during last year's assignment protecting the President had to been hard for Tim to accept. The President had tried to explain that he needed it to look like he was still in residence. If he had taken his personal agent, it would have been obvious the President was not in the White House. Even discussing it with Tim could have posed a risk.

The explanation had fallen on deaf ears. Tim tried to accept the reasons, but the news media reporting on the internal terrorism plot uncovered by the President and Agent Wayne Mitchell even continues, in some ways, to this day. His standing with his fellow agents also took a hit. They were less than understanding of how a lead agent, assigned to the President, was not with him during such an important event. They even wondered aloud if the President didn't trust him…something unacceptable to a fellow agent. An agent cannot serve effectively if his loyalty and dedication comes into question. Tim knows Wayne had no say in the matter, but he still cannot help resenting him.

"Tim," Wayne begins, "can I talk with you a minute?"

"What?" Tim reacts sarcastically. "Do you want to ask me if you can tuck the President in?"

Wayne lets the remark slide. "I was wondering, when you went through Scott Bender's office after he died, where all did you look?"

Tim stops sipping his coffee and stares coldly at Wayne. "What makes you think I was ever looking through Bender's office?"

A moment passes as both men size each other up. Tim gives a half smile and shakes his head, "He told you. Why doesn't he just have you replace me if he is that hot for you?"

Wayne presses. "I need to know."

Tim turns his back to Wayne and ignores him.

Wayne pushes harder, "Who did you call when you couldn't find the ledger?"

Tim stiffens noticeably but continues to watch television and sip coffee.

Wayne tries one more push. "Was it your brother?"

That does it. Tim jumps up and rushes Wayne. Wayne dodges the first lunge, but a reverse sweep kick takes Wayne's legs out from under him as he hits the ground hard. Tim follows with a sidekick to the head that luckily doesn't catch Wayne squarely. Wayne rolls to get out of the line of the next attack and counters with a rising sidekick to Tim's midsection as he rushes Wayne. The kick lifts Tim off the ground and lands him onto one of the coffee tables. He hits hard on his back but is able to roll off quickly.

He struggles to catch the breath knocked out of him from the kick. Both agents now face each other. Quicker than the thought process, both men are attacking and defending. Thrust and side punches are deflected as efficiently as delivered. Equally trained in hand-to-hand combat, neither gives an opening to the other. Needing to end this quickly, Wayne takes a risk when Tim throws a thrust punch, catching it in mid-motion while stepping to the side. The timing on this has to be perfect. All in one motion, he lifts Tim off his feet and throws him over his hip onto the floor. Maintaining his hold on his arm and wrist, he steps around Tim's prone body while straightening his arm in a reverse position and using the armlock to push down on the shoulder. Wayne then places his knee onto Tim's back.

Having done this himself to a number of other people, Tim knows the fight is over and he has lost. Even the slightest movement causes excruciating pain in the arm and shoulder. Wayne and Tim use a moment to try to catch their breath. It's harder, though, for Tim with the side of his face pressed against the floor.

"I'll ask you again," Wayne begins. "Who did you call when you didn't find the list?"

"No one." Tim struggles with the words with his mouth against the floor.

Wayne knows he has to follow this through. Torn between needing desperately to get answers and hoping a fellow agent isn't dirty, Wayne begins to apply pressure to the arm and shoulder socket. Tim tries to resist the tremendous pain but knows he'll pass out soon and possibly lose full use of his arm if he doesn't stop Wayne.

"I did not call any one," Tim shouts as he waits to see if Wayne releases some of the pressure on his arm and shoulder. Slight as it is, it's enough for Tim to hope his arm will survive. The reprieve is fleeting, though, as Wayne again begins to bear down on the arm and shoulder.

"But you were right," Tim finally yells out just as his arm socket is about to dislocate.

Wayne immediately releases most of the pressure on the arm and shoulder, but not the hold.

"I didn't call my brother," Tim reluctantly continues, "but we had lunch yesterday and I mentioned to him in passing that the President had me look through Bender's things for a ledger of some kind. That was it. The President never told me what it was or why he needed it, only that it would be a book with names and descriptions in it. That's all I told Mike. I just said it in passing, I should have known better. We didn't talk of it further. I didn't think I had said that much. Heck, he's a fellow agent. There was no malice intended."

Wayne slowly releases Tim's arm and allows him to get off the floor. Tim moves to the chair he was sitting in when Wayne came in and rubs his injured arm and shoulder. Wayne struggles to argue with Tim's logic that he was only making innocent conversation with his brother, but agents are sworn to extreme secrecy when it comes to those they are assigned to guard. It will be up to a review board to decide if Tim's indiscretion is enough to relieve him of his duties.

Wayne looks at Tim. "I hope a conversation with a brother isn't what has caused our current problem, but I need to know where your brother is right now."

"Wayne," Tim pleads, "how could what little I told my brother be reason for this problem you mentioned?"

"Obviously," Wayne points out, "I'm not about to get into the same type of conversation that you got in with your brother. It's enough to say that if you don't tell me where your brother is, obstruction of an agent in the line of duty will be added to your current trouble."

Tim knows what little is left of his career depends on how he helps Wayne now. "One request, though." Tim looks hard at Wayne. "I need to go with you."

Wayne stares back in disbelief. "You could be facing federal charges, and you think I would trust you to come with me? Even if I did, how could I trust you to back me against your brother?"

"I know what I did was wrong," Tim explains, "but you have to know I didn't do it against anyone, especially the President. My only hope now is to help correct what problem this may have caused. If my brother is involved, my loyalty to my oath and country far outweighs any loyalty to my brother."

"Let's say I consider this," Wayne hesitantly responds. "I'd have to discuss this with the President and get his approval."

"Well, it's either that or the President still finds out and I'm under arrest," Tim humbly points out.

Wayne bows his head and shakes it because he truly doesn't know what to do. Looking back at Tim, he reaches for the secure phone to the

Oval Office that is in the Secret Service room and places the call. In just seconds, Wayne is talking to the President. Wayne decides to let Tim listen to the conversation.

"Mr. President, I just had a long conversation with Agent Peters and I feel he can help." There is a pause as Wayne listens to what the President's response is. "Yes, sir, but I'd like to have him with me for the rest of my required time on this." There is another pause. "I understand sir. If it is all right, I'll need to bring him somewhat up to speed on what I am doing." Another small pause. "No, that will not be a problem. Thank you, sir."

Wayne hangs up the phone and looks over at Tim. "I don't agree with what you did, but it's hard for me to condemn you too. I feel you're a good agent, Tim, so I'm willing to let you prove yourself and so is the President."

"I won't let you or the President down."

"Now," Wayne asks, "where is your brother?"

Thirteen

Trust

In a cold, dark room, Kathy and Taylor sit hugging each other as they try to make themselves believe they will be all right. Their trust in God comforts them greatly, but they still would like to know why this has happened. The speed in which everything took place at the police station overwhelmed the officers so completely they were helpless to defend themselves. So fast was the attack that the officers barely stood up before the shots found their mark. Seconds later, with hoods over the women's heads, the attackers moved Kathy and Taylor from the station to a car. They then traveled at a high rate of speed, hitting ruts in the road hard before making it to a paved road.

The women have no idea where they are. The hoods stayed on until they were in the room they now sit. They know it took about 30 minutes to get here and they are in a lower floor room, because they went down a set of stairs. There are no windows and no lights except for a sliver coming from under the door. Their eyes have yet to adjust to the darkness.

After being in the room for a while, they can make out dark outlines of file cabinets and shelving along the walls. As their eyes adjust more, Kathy stands up and starts to feel around for a light switch. She finally locates one, but when she flips up the switch, nothing happens. She returns to sit next to her daughter, hugs her tightly again, tells her everything will be all right…and prays.

Back at the White House, Tim tells Wayne where Mike is, and Wayne explains what happened at the Bender estate earlier but doesn't reveal what the ledger contains. Tim calls Mike to make sure he is where he was and says he wants to drop buy and visit. He's conveniently only a block away, at The Willard. Wayne can't help but smile at this since that same location was where he had hidden a year ago while he looked for the missing President.

Tim explains that Mike is in town as part of the advance team for the arrival of former president Shane Osburn. Osburn, along with numerous other dignitaries and celebrities, will be coming to Washington for the funerals of Vice-President Dave Charles and chief of staff Scott Bender. Mike became part of the security team of Shane Osburn after he left the presidency, filling the vacancy left by Austin Ivers.

It only takes a few minutes for the two agents to walk out of the White House grounds and down the street to The Willard. The Willard had become a grand hotel when the Willard brothers purchased the property in 1850. It has hosted almost every president since Franklin Pierce in 1853.

As Wayne and Tim enter through the front entrance of the hotel, Wayne notices and waves to a dear friend, Sheri Lee, the concierge, who greatly helped him last year during his hunt for the President. They then turn right toward the elevators, which they take up to the fifth floor. From there they make their way to the corner room at the end of the hall where Mike is staying.

Knocking on the door, they wait for Mike to let them in. They can hear some sounds coming from inside the room followed by the door opening up. As the door opens, Mike's happy face changes quickly once he sees that Tim is not alone. He ushers them both into the room. Mike is maybe a little shorter than Tim, probably 6 feet 5 inches, but just as solidly built, with a chiseled face and frame and jet black hair. After handshakes and some small pleasantries, Wayne gets to the point.

"Mike, I wish this visit was just us coming by to see a fellow agent, but it's more than that." Wayne looks over at Tim and back at Mike. "I understand that you and Tim had a conversation during lunch the other day where Tim mentioned that President Anders had asked him to look through chief of staff Bender's office to try to find some sort of ledger."

Mike looks a little confused. "I really don't remember that much of what we talked about, but if Tim says he did, then I guess he did."

"Well," Wayne says, "what I need from you is who you relayed that bit of information to."

Mike reacts defensively. "I didn't tell anyone. I said, I don't even remember him discussing it with me."

"Mike," Wayne explains, "this isn't about protecting Tim. He has already confessed. It's now about protecting two innocent, helpless people."

Mike shakes his head. "I can't tell you anything more than what I already told you."

Wayne turns to Tim. "You have two minutes to change how this is going." Wayne moves to a chair near a window.

Tim stands and slowly walks over to Mike. "Please, Mike, I need you to tell us who you told. Too many things have happened since I told you to just chalk it up to coincidence."

Mike shakes his head and is about to deny it again when Tim speaks. "Many people have died, Mike. And Mrs. Bender and her daughter have been kidnapped."

Mike's head slumps down and a strong silence takes over the room. Only moments pass, but Wayne cannot wait any longer. He stands to do a little stronger form of interrogation.

But Wayne hasn't yet taken a step when Mike blurts out, "I, like Tim, just mentioned it in passing during breakfast this morning with another agent. We were meeting about Osburn's pending visit here and I just made a short comment about what Tim had said."

"Who did you mention it to?" Wayne demanded.

"I'm sure he wouldn't have done anything that would have caused what you both are speaking of," Mike began, trying to fend off getting his fellow agent in trouble.

Wayne has reached the end of his patience. "WHO?" he shouts.

"Agent Austin Ivers," Mike mumbles.

Wayne was afraid of that. He was hoping for another name that could give them a lead to where the women are. Instead, all he has is the name of someone he already knows about and is dead. Wayne turns and sits back down in the chair and shakes his head.

Mike and Tim look confused at Wayne's reaction to what Mike just said and stare over at him, hoping for an answer.

Wayne eventually looks up and sighs. "Well, gentlemen, Agent Ivers was killed earlier today after his involvement in a number of deaths. I'm now back at a dead end."

A few moments pass before the silence is broken. "Maybe not," Mike hesitantly offers. "After finishing breakfast, I went to the restroom. As I returned, I overheard Austin talking on the phone to someone. I don't know who it was, but you said he was killed. If you can locate his cell phone or call record, I could pinpoint what call he made and to whom."

Wayne remembers he had left Ivers' body at the police station at Sandy Point State Park, but when he went back, he didn't see it anywhere. The killers had taken the body with them and obviously, Ivers' cell phone, which was probably in a pocket.

But Mike's right...we can get access to his call record. Wayne begins to leave the hotel room alone when Tim calls out to him.

"Wayne, you can use our help."

"Guys," Wayne struggles to be kind, "you've helped me, but remember I'm also in this position because you both seem unable to keep your mouths shut. I can't afford to have anything jeopardize my saving the two people you have so carelessly put in harm's way." Wayne heads for the room door.

"I promised I wouldn't let you down, and I meant it," Tim reminds Wayne.

Wayne stops as he reaches for the doorknob. "Yes, but your brother didn't, and I will need you to stay with him and make sure he doesn't break your promise."

"Hey," Mike blurts out, "I know we screwed up, but we're still agents, bound by our oath. I give you my word that we are with you to the end, if you'll have us."

Wayne begins to turn the doorknob, then stops again. A few

seconds pass. "Just don't give me a reason to shoot you." He holds the door open.

Not wanting to give Wayne any time to change his mind, Tim and Mike rush through the door. Less than ten minutes later, they are back in the Secret Service office of the White House, trying to get a response from their inquiry into Austin Ivers' cell phone records. It only takes a few minutes, using the extensive files available to the Secret Service department, before the information needed is on the computer screen. Looking through the records Mike points to the call made just before he came back from the bathroom at the restaurant.

Since it is now nearly 11:30 p.m., Wayne pulls up a list of cell phone company regional managers and goes through it until he comes up with the person he needs. Right next to the name is the home phone number. He picks up the office's secure line to make the call. Wayne hears a sleepy voice after a few rings. Wayne apologizes for waking the man, but explains who he is and what his request is. To expedite the authorization process, Wayne gives the man the phone number to the White House switchboard and tells him to call it and ask for the Secret Service office. Wayne hangs up and a couple of minutes later the phone rings next to him. Not five minutes after that, Wayne has the name he needs.

After thanking the man for his help, Wayne hangs up and turns to Tim and Mike. "Do either of you know a Garrett Coffman?"

Fourteen

Dark Figures

The door slowly opens, sending a growing beam of light into the dark room holding the Bender women. Having been in the dark for what seems like about an hour to them, it takes awhile for their eyes to adjust to the new source of light. Because the light is coming from behind those now entering the room, all the women can make out are dark figures. The first of those, a tall man, quickly stands off to the side once he is in the room. The next to enter is a tall, heavyset figure of a man who walks over to the women. No other light but the light from the door entrance is in the room and the heavyset man makes sure that light remains behind him.

"I'm sorry for all the inconveniences you've had to suffer through today," the man very politely says, "but you can end this very quickly and be on your way. All we want is the ledger that your husband left behind when he died, Mrs. Bender."

Kathy struggles to make out any features of the man's face, but the strong light coming from behind him makes his face a dark wash.

"I wish I knew what you are asking for," Kathy replies, "but I know nothing of any ledger he may or may not have kept. I'd give it to you if I could."

The man motions to the other man who had entered the room first. That man moves toward the women, reaches down, grabs Taylor's arm, and pulls her to her feet roughly while placing a hood back over her head.

"Mrs. Bender," the man continues, "don't let my calm manner deceive you, for I won't hesitate a moment to have my men hurt your daughter."

"I don't have the ledger and I don't know where it is," Kathy pleads.

The man motions again, and Taylor is forcibly taken from the room.

"Mom!" Taylor yells out as she leaves Kathy's sight.

"You have ten minutes to reconsider," the man states. "Your memory better kick in soon. And don't think you can tell me you gave it to Wayne Mitchell, for he would have given it up back at the house to protect you and your daughter. You really should do no less."

He walks toward the bright light of the doorway and closes the door behind him.

Kathy jumps up and rushes the door, screaming, "Please, don't do this! I'd tell you if I knew!" She pounds on the door.

Crying uncontrollably, Kathy walks back in the dark, to where she was sitting. She hits the chair with her knee since it is now again so dark she cannot see anything. She then sits down…alone.

"Oh God, please help us," she calls out into the dark.

Kathy struggles to stay calm, trying as hard as she can to remember something, anything that she could tell the men, but the fear for her daughter keeps creeping into her mind and clouding her thought process. The minutes tick past. She can't remember anything her husband might have mentioned about the ledger. She once again prays for help, crying out in the darkness. All of a sudden, a memory comes out of nowhere. She jumps up, runs to the door, and pounds on it as she yells that she knows where it is. She keeps pounding on the door until she hears the door unlocking. She steps back as the door opens slowly.

As soon as she sees the guard's silhouette she blurts out, "My husband once told me he had to open a lockbox for some special things he wanted to keep safe. He said it had nothing to do with family things, but he wanted me to know about it just in case something happened to him. It was about four years ago he told me, and I just forgot it since it had nothing to do with the family."

The guard pushes her back farther into the dark room as the other man appears at the doorway. He stands there for a few seconds before responding, "Well, where is the lockbox?"

Kathy was afraid he would ask that. It was all she could do to remember that Scott had mentioned the lockbox at all. "Just give me a few minutes to remember." She desperately tries to compose herself. Seconds pass, and she sees the man is getting impatient. "I know it's a bank close to the White House," Kathy blurts out. "If you could get me a phone book, I could go through it. I'm sure when I see the name, I'll recognize it."

The man cannot decide if she is stalling or truly has the answer. Knowing it probably wouldn't serve any purpose to threaten her with harming her child anymore, he gives her the benefit of the doubt and tells the guard next to him to get a phone book.

"Please, can you bring back my daughter?" Kathy begs.

"If what you say is the truth, then when we retrieve the ledger you will be reunited with her. But if the ledger is not where you tell us, then…" The man leaves Kathy to imagine what would happen next.

The guard returns and hands the phone book to Kathy. She quickly starts to turn the pages, but stops and looks up. "Is there any way I could get some more light?"

"Stand up, turn around, and with your back to me, walk backwards to the door. You will have enough light then," the man points out.

Kathy does as instructed. As she gets closer to the door, she soon has enough light to read the bank names in the phone book. Having no real idea of the bank's name, she starts with the *A*s.

In a different part of the building, Taylor sits in another room. This room, though, has a working light switch, which Taylor discovered right after they pushed her in. The room has some chairs and a table; possibly it's used as a conference room. Taylor is too upset to sit, so she paces continuously around the table while she thinks of what she should do. She had tried to hide her cell phone in her bra, but that turned out to be the first place the men that took her searched. In all the chaos at the house, her mom had forgotten hers. Probably better, since it would belong to these men now.

Taylor hears the door unlock, and a hand reaches in and turns off the light to the room. "Keep this light off," demands the voice of the silhouette at the door. "If I see it on again, your mother will suffer for it." The door slams shut.

The guard then walks back to his chair outside the room holding Taylor and sits down. As he leans the chair back, another guard walks up.

"Coffman says we are to keep these two separated, but no harm is to come to them, understand?" the other guard explains.

The guard in the chair nods but isn't pleased. He had hoped to have some fun with the daughter.

The other guard continues, "Also, plan on us being here all night, but we'll move out first thing in the morning."

The sitting guard again nods as the other guard walks back to where the mother and Coffman are.

Kathy is still trying to come up with the name of the bank that has the lockbox.

All of a sudden, Kathy yells, "EagleBank," as her finger points to it in the phone book. "I remember Scott said to think of the eagle of the Presidential Seal to remember it."

Coffman grabs the phone book from Kathy, "What branch?" he barks impatiently.

Kathy searches her mind for the answer, but she cannot remember. "I don't know, but as I said, it would be near the White House."

Coffman looks at the branch listing for EagleBank and sees the one he needs: DuPont Circle branch. He motions for the guard as he turns to leave. Just before he steps out of the door, he looks back at Kathy. "We'll be expecting you to get us access to the box tomorrow morning. Let's hope nothing goes wrong, understand?"

Then the door closes and the darkness sets in again. Kathy can only hope and pray that her daughter is safe.

Down the hall, Taylor is doing the same thing, praying her mother is safe as she sits in her dark room.

Outside Taylor's door, the guard assigned to her watches as Coffman leaves the mother and heads upstairs. He is not happy having to stay up all night, especially now that Coffman cancelled the fun with the women. He leans his chair back against the wall again and stares blankly forward when he feels something protruding out of his front pocket. He reaches down, pulls the object out of his pocket, and lazily brings it to eye level.

He suddenly remembers that when he had patted down the daughter, he'd found her cell phone stuck in her bra. He brings it to his nose; he can still smell her perfume on it. He cannot help but fantasize being in the room with her now. He starts to put the phone back in his pocket when an idea comes to him. If Coffman is going to make him stay down here all night and take away his fun, he'll just make some fun for himself. He turns the phone on and starts making a call. A few moments later, he is talking to an old friend in Hawaii he hasn't talked to for a year. *Heck, it's not even 9 p.m. there,* he thinks to himself.

Fifteen

He Has Heard the Name

Wayne waits to hear from Mike or Tim if either knows who Garrett Coffman is. Neither says anything at first, but after a few seconds, Mike acknowledges he's heard the name.

"I heard Shane Osburn mention his name," Mike offers.

"When would that have been?" Wayne asks, a little surprised.

"About a month ago," Mike replies.

Wayne pushes for more information. Mike resists, stating confidentiality issues but Wayne will have none of that.

"We are talking about a sitting President's needs now and your oath to him and this country," Wayne explains. "Anything less than that gets in back of the line."

"Osburn was talking to Ivers," Mike says, "and I was just coming into the room as Osburn said the name. They stopped talking when they saw me. Later, I asked some questions of the other agents who had been with Osburn for a while. All I could get was that Coffman worked for the Osburn administration for a short time before being let go. What he did or why he was given his walking papers, I have no idea."

Wayne takes a seat near where he was standing and shakes his head in disbelief. How has he not heard of this Coffman person? Suddenly the phone in the Secret Service office rings. Wayne gets up and covers the room quickly to pick up the phone. On the other end is Wayne's friend at the FBI, telling him that one of the cell phone numbers Wayne gave him is active and operating about thirty miles north of the White House in the small town of Dayton, Maryland. According to his friend, the phone is stationary, but he'll monitor it and call Wayne's cell phone if it moves. Wayne writes down the number that'is active and the coordinates, thanks his friend, and hangs up.

Comparing the number with the two he had given his friend, he knows what phone it matches. "We have a location on Taylor's phone," he announces to Tim and Mike. "Let's go."

All three head to the weapons cabinet and grab various large caliber rifles and gas canisters along with mouth-size oxygen cylinders, night-vision goggles, and a set of heavy gauge wire cutters. They then check their handguns to make sure they are fully loaded. Before they leave, they take extra rounds, just in case.

It's now after 1 a.m., and the traffic is very light, but it will still take them nearly thirty minutes to get to Dayton. The coordinates that Wayne was given are the intersection of Ten Oaks, Green Bridge, and Linthicum roads. Wayne has never been to the town, and Tim and Mike confirm that is true for them too. Within 10 minutes, driving as fast as they dare through downtown Washington, they have made it to interstate 495 and soon will be merging into I-95 north. That will take them to state road 32 north, which then takes them to W. Linden Church road, which intersects with Ten Oaks. That will take them to the intersection they need.

While driving, Wayne looks over at Tim in the front seat next to him. Wayne has never worked with either of the Peters' brothers, and now they all are going into harm's way. He hopes he can count on them. He normally would welcome the additional help, but their reason for being here is not as noble as Wayne would have liked, though he expects their actions to be that of the highly trained agents they are.

At speeds approaching 100 miles per hour, it only takes 5 minutes to travel the 12 miles to 32 north. It will only be a few more minutes before they get off onto W. Linden Church road. Wayne quickly slows down as he sees the exit sign for the road. Less than a half mile on Linden Church, they come to the Ten Oaks road and turn right, heading to Dayton. Only a couple of miles takes them right to the intersection of the three roads Wayne's friend told him to go to. He notices that many acres of woods surround the area.

On opposite sides of the intersection are commercial buildings—one small, another of medium size. The medium-size building has many tractor trailer rigs parked in the lot; the smaller one has a couple of vehicles parked in its lot that look very much like the black, late model sedans that were part of the assault on the Bender estate. Wayne pulls into the larger building's parking lot and turns the car so the smaller building is plainly visible. He sees there are lights on in the building. The peripheral buildings near the main one do not have any lights on. For now, Wayne will focus just on the main building.

"Men," Wayne starts, "we are going to make our way over to that building across the street. What I need from you both is to know that I can count on you to follow through with this to the end."

Both brothers confirm their commitment to him.

"Then I need you both go across the street and make your way around the back of that building and wait until you hear this gas canister go off," Wayne holds out the canister, "or shooting, whichever is first. Then I want you to cut the power to the building. And remember, there may be two women hostages in there."

Tim and Mike open the car doors and slip out, each carrying the necessary equipment of night-vision goggles and oxygen cylinders, along with assault rifle and their standard-issue handgun. Wayne watches until both are behind the building before he gets out of the car, also carrying an assault rifle in addition to his handgun and night-vision goggles. Quickly and quietly, he makes his way to the front porch. Wayne peers around a front window frame just in time to see a barrel of a gun. He ducks back just before the explosion of the gun blast. He immediately knows that he, or one of the others, must have triggered an alarm sensor.

Inside, Wayne hears a lot of commotion as the power goes off, then the crash of glass as Wayne assumes it is Tim and Mike entering the building. There are numerous bursts of gunfire coming from inside. Wayne puts on his night-vision goggles and inserts the oxygen cylinder mouthpiece into his mouth. He then activates the gas canister and throws it through the window next to him. A second later, there is an explosion and smoke billows from the broken window. Wayne hurls himself through the same window, breaking the rest of the glass out of it.

Mo Mower heads down the stairs of the building as he follows Garrett Coffman while protecting his rear. As they approach the bottom of the stairs, Garrett yells to the guard watching the doors of the two rooms holding the women to get them out and follow him out the back passage. The emergency lighting has covered the basement with enough light to get around in.

The guard had heard the gunfire and had turned off Taylor's cell phone before Garrett had made his way down the stairs. He immediately opens the daughter's door first since he is there, then runs to Kathy's door and unlocks it. As the women leave their rooms, Mo hears someone at the top stairs and sends a few rounds of gunfire up the stairwell to force back anyone trying to come down.

Taylor tries to take advantage of the turmoil by making a break for it, but the guard grabs Taylor's arm and drags her behind him. He heads for the back passage that will take them out into the woods where a camouflaged barn houses a number of vehicles for their escape. Garrett moves toward Kathy but misses her arm as she recoils away from him. She loses her balance and falls against the wall. Garrett reaches out again just as a gas canister explodes at the foot of the stairs, causing him to draw back his hand to cover his nose and mouth. Kathy runs back into the room that had held her prisoner, but now it protects her. The darkness of the room envelops her as she hides between some shelving. Garrett considers going into the room after her, but self-preservation kicks in as the overwhelming gas from the canister starts to fill the area.

Mo, too, is starting to feel the effects of the gas. He grabs his boss by the arm. "We have to get out of here."

Both men run to the back passage door. As they pass through, Mo stops for a second to punch in a code that activates a timer. Red diodes show a time of one minute. He pushes *Enter* and the timer starts counting down: *59, 58, 57...* Mo then runs to catch up with Garrett.

Wayne dives down the stairs into the room now filled with gas. The night-vision goggles keep the harmful gas from his eyes and the small oxygen cylinder keep the fumes out of his lungs. As he hits the ground, he rolls and waits to see if he attracts any fire.

Nothing comes. As he did upstairs, Wayne shoots out the emergency lights in the area to allow the night-vision goggles to work. He can see no one down here.

"Kathy, Taylor," Wayne calls out. There is no reply. He calls the names again. This time he hears coughing coming from across the room. He makes his way in that direction, prepared to fire at anything threatening. Another cough comes from inside a room directly in front of him. He calls the women's names again and hears a struggling reply from Kathy, "I'm in here."

Wayne rushes in and locates her quickly with the night-goggles. She is slumped over and coughing violently from the fumes flowing into her room. Wayne immediately picks her up in his arms and rushes her up the stairs. Taking steps two at a time, he reaches the top of the stairs and carries her outside to the fresh air.

Tim and Mike, seeing Wayne run past them, follow him outside since they have killed everyone else.

Wayne lays Kathy down on the grass as she continues to cough violently, then takes the oxygen cylinder from his mouth. "You guys stay with Kathy. I need to go back in and see if Taylor is somewhere in the basement."

"You stay here," Tim tells Wayne, "Mike and I will go."

Both brothers immediately turn and run toward the house. They both hit the first stair at the same time when an explosion rips through the building, sending the brothers hurling backward nearly twenty feet as debris falls all around. The force of the explosion even knocks Wayne down next to Kathy while pieces of the structure rain down on them. Wayne leans over Kathy to protect her as the wreckage continues to fall.

A few seconds later Wayne looks up from Kathy. He first sees Tim and Mike, both shaken and slowly trying to get their bearings as they struggle to stand up. Wayne is glad for that, but then a terrible feeling overtakes him as he realizes he was not able to save Taylor.

He turns to Kathy and holds her tightly. "I'm so sorry."

"I'm okay Wayne," Kathy informs him as she coughs a last bit.

Wayne, realizing she doesn't know Taylor's fate, explains, "I meant about Taylor."

Kathy looks confused, then it dawns on her what he's thinking, "No, I saw them take her out a back way. I'm sure she's still alive. They tried to take me too, but I was able to get away and hide during the gunfire."

Wayne is relieved as he leans back on the ground to recover from the emotional rollercoaster he's just ridden. Out of the corner of his eye, he sees the brothers moving toward him, but Tim stumbles and falls to his knees. Wayne sits up as Mike turns to his brother and kids him about being out of shape. Tim looks down at his chest, then up at Mike.

The darkness of the night keeps everyone from seeing what Tim now knows: a long, shard of glass from the explosion has entered his chest and punctured his heart. Tim initially thought the pain was just from landing hard after flying nearly twenty feet. However, as he struggled to his feet, his breath became very ragged and the pain in his chest overwhelmed him to the point of his legs giving out from under him. He has seen this type of wound before and knows what to expect. Tim holds out his hand to his brother, and Mike kneels down and grasps it tightly.

"Mike," Tim talks through his labored breathing, "you're not a part of any of this, are you?"

"Of course not," Mike answers passionately.

"Then don't let our mistake hurt anyone else. Promise me you'll make this right for us."

"I will."

Tim looks over at Wayne. "He's a good agent. He'll make this right." Then he gazes at Mike. "I've always been proud of you."

Mike hugs his brother to him as Tim coughs violently, then goes limp in his arms. Mike hugs him awhile longer, then lowers him to the ground.

Kathy covers her face and cries.

Wayne walks over to Mike, puts his arm around him, and asks him what he wants to do.

Mike continues to look down at his brother. "Can we take my brother back to Washington before going after them?"

Wayne agrees and helps Mike pick his brother up and take him over to the car while Kathy follows close behind.

A high-powered rifle bears down on the group below, aimed, in particular, at Kathy. Just beyond the woods, up on a bluff, Mo has fashioned a makeshift gun stand on the hood of the car they drove out of the camouflaged barn and has been following Kathy's movement through the night-vision scope on his USMC M40A3 sniper rifle. The same rifle he used earlier to silence Austin Ivers. Garrett gets out of the car and motions to the guard in the back seat with Taylor to come too. Garrett is about to give Mo the order to kill Kathy. If she isn't going to give him the ledger, she isn't going to give it to anyone.

"I have her," Mo says. He's ready to make the kill.

Taylor, dragged over to the two men by the guard, hears Mo. Seeing what is about to happen, she screams out, "Stop! I'm the one who has the ledger. My mom knows nothing about it."

Both Garrett and Mo continue to look out over the woods to the intended target as the fire from the explosion illuminates her nicely.

"I'll take you to it now, but you can't harm my mother," Taylor demands.

"Sir, we only have a few more seconds for the target," Mo informs Garrett.

Garrett turns to Taylor and stares at her. Does she really have the ledger, or is it just an attempt to save her mother? "Where is it?"

Taylor hesitates for a couple of seconds, then shouts, "At my college!"

Garrett tries to read Taylor's face for any sign it is a lie but is unable to do so.

"Hold your shot, Mo," Garrett reluctantly instructs.

Mo slowly releases the pressure on the trigger of the rifle and backs away.

"Young lady, don't think you have saved your mother entirely," Garrett points out. "Be sure, if you don't produce the ledger, both of you will die."

At that same moment, Kathy gets into the front seat of the car with Wayne while Mike sits in the back holding Tim's body. Wayne pulls the car out of the parking lot and heads back to Washington.

Sixteen

What College?

Taylor is back in Garrett's car, next to the guard. Just before getting in, though, she noticed her cell phone protruding out of the guard's right front pocket. Once in the car, Taylor only goes in about halfway on the seat, forcing the guard to sit right next to her when he gets in. Taylor puts her hand along the top of his leg as if to push off him to slide farther down the seat. This is enough contact to distract the guard's senses and allow Taylor's other hand to pull her cell phone out of the guard's pocket without him noticing. It's a cheap, pickpocket trick, but effective, especially when done by beautiful women. Taught this by her college roommate to prove how easy it is to distract men, they would test it during parties and always have a good laugh when they gave back the wallets lifted from unsuspecting male partygoers. Taylor palms her cell phone and slips it into her pocket to wait for the right time to turn it on.

The front car doors open and both Garrett and Mo get into the seats, Mo behind the wheel and Garrett in the passenger seat. Garrett then turns around to face Taylor and says firmly, "Okay, young lady, what college are we going to?"

Taylor cannot think of anything else to say to stall them, "Wisconsin," Taylor reluctantly answers.

Garrett Coffman smiles, "That's funny. I went to a college not too far from there."

Back in Washington, Wayne pulls into the city morgue after about a 30-minute drive. Mike understands that time is of the essence and the people at the morgue will tend to Tim properly until he can make other arrangements. Mike and Wayne go into the morgue to explain the situation. The city morgue has worked with agents often and understands how to handle delicate situations for the government. A few minutes later, the staff carries Tim into the morgue with Mike's help as Wayne waits in the car with Kathy. Soon Mike comes out and gets into the back seat of the car again.

"Let's go," is all Mike says.

Wayne starts the car to head back to the White House. Going back works best for Wayne, too. He needs to report to the President and leave Kathy in secure surroundings. He can no longer fear that more Secret Service Agents are involved. If there were, they would never try anything in the White House, especially in the President's private quarters, which is where Wayne is going to ask the President to house her. They only have to travel a short distance before they are inside the White House grounds.

All three make their way into the White House, where Wayne tells a security staff member to have the President informed they are here and that it is an emergency. Since it's after 2 a.m., the President has retired for the night, but Wayne insists the President know they are here. The staff member calls up to the private quarters, where a Secret Service Agent answers the phone. The President had told this agent that Wayne might try to contact him and to wake him if he does. Only a short time passes before an agent comes to take them up the stairs to the private quarters of the first family.

The President greets the three when they reach the top of the stairs. His face shows his surprise, though, to see Mike Peters instead of Tim. The President directs them across from the stairs to the room called the Treaty Room, called that since 1962 when Jackie Kennedy had it restored and named it for all the treaties that had been signed there. Now the President uses it as his private office. The President motions the three to enter the room before him while he stays back to give privacy instructions to his attending agent. With a nod of understanding from the agent, the President heads into the Treaty Room.

The three stand as the President enters, but he asks them to sit back down as he walks to his desk chair and sits. "It's so good to see you all, especially you, Kathy. But where are Tim and Taylor?"

Mike looks at Wayne and then the President. "Tim didn't make it, sir."

"Oh my." The President's voice cracks a little. "What happened?"

"Mr. President," Wayne explains, "with the help of Mike, we located where they had taken Kathy and Taylor, but they had the building protected with warning sensors. After an exchange of gunfire, I was able to bring Kathy out, but they were able to escape with Taylor."

"Oh Kathy, I'm so sorry."

Wayne continues, "When Tim and Mike went back into the building, hoping to get Taylor back, the building exploded, killing Tim. On the way here we took Tim's body to the city morgue."

The President slumps, devastated by the news.

"I'd like Kathy to stay here in the White House, if that would be possible," Wayne adds.

"Of course," the President responds, "that goes without saying. Kathy, we'll put you in the Queen's Bedroom just down the hall." The President calls down to the housekeeping staff quarters and has them make the necessary arrangements. He then goes out of the room and instructs the agent at the door to have protection assigned to Kathy. Returning to the Treaty Room, he again sits behind his desk.

"Gentlemen, we have to get Taylor back safely," the President makes clear its importance. "That has become your first priority. Only after that is anything else a concern. Mike, I now transfer you to my personal protection staff until this is accomplished, if that is all right with you."

"Of course, Mr. President."

"I will have someone contact former president Osburn later this morning to inform him of this temporary assignment. Since time is of the essence from now on, is there anything else I can do for you both before you head out?"

Realizing that was their cue, Wayne and Mike both stand up, "No, Mr. President," Wayne speaks for both agents. They say good-bye to Kathy.

The President stands and makes his way from behind his desk to walk the agents to the door. "I'm counting on you both to save her."

"Yes, sir," Wayne answers. He reaches into his pocket and pulls out the lockbox key that Nancy Roberts had given him. "Mr. President," Wayne whispers, "when it is safe, this might be where you can find what you need, with the help of Kathy."

The President softly says he understands, takes the lockbox key, and shakes Wayne's hand. Wayne then leaves with Mike right behind.

In a couple of minutes, they are in their car and leaving the White House grounds. They both know they have to get back to Dayton and sift through the debris to find anything that might help them locate where Taylor might be. On the way, Wayne calls the FBI contact he used earlier and asks him to find out what he can about Garrett Coffman. The man agrees to do what he can and will call Wayne back if he finds something. About 25 minutes later, they are on Ten Oaks road in Dayton.

As they approach the building, they see a number of police, ambulance, and fire vehicles on the scene. When they get close, an officer directs them to another road, but Wayne stops and rolls down his driver's side window and shows him his Secret Service badge.

"We have been sent by the President to secure this site for national security reasons," Wayne tells the officer. "I need to talk to who is in charge."

"That would be Sergeant Burdett. I'll get him," the officer offers.

A minute later the sergeant approaches Wayne's car. "How can I help you?"

Wayne again shows his Secret Service badge, "I'm Secret Service Agent Wayne Mitchell and this is Agent Mike Peters. We need your men and the fire department to pull back from the area until further notice."

"I'm sorry, Agent Mitchell," the sergeant replies, "but there are bodies in there and we're in the middle of a potential homicide investigation. I'm going to have to ask you to wait until that has run its course before we can let you in."

"Sergeant," Wayne barked, "let me shorten your investigation immensely. Myself and Agent Peters are the ones who killed them, and if you don't back away from the scene you will be obstructing a federal agent in the line of duty and will go to prison if I don't shoot you first. Now, this comes straight from the President of the United States and I would recommend you call the White House operator to confirm this before you and your men are sharing a cell in your own jail."

The sergeant steps back from the car and for a moment considers ignoring the agent's threat, then thinks better of it and tells the officer next to him to bring everyone out of the building and give the two agents free reign. A couple of minutes later, Wayne can see the officers and fire personnel coming out of the building. The agents quickly enter the burned-out building.

Looking around, Wayne and Mike see the huge amount of damage caused by the explosion and subsequent fire. Coffman knew what he was doing when he set the building to explode. The upper floors, mostly just charred remains, appear to have housed the offices, so they start with what is left of them. After some extensive sifting, they find two damaged computers that might have a chance at giving up some of their information. Just in case, they also retrieve the hard drive from two more seriously damaged computers found in pieces and badly burned. After about an hour of searching, they are unable to locate anything more that might help.

Taking the computers to the car, Wayne tells the sergeant that they can take over the investigation again. The sergeant just smiles and yells that everyone can get back to work as Wayne and Mike head back into Washington to have the computer hard drives analyzed. Wayne again calls his FBI friend and tells him he needs another favor. His only question for Wayne is, "Don't you ever sleep?" Wayne laughs and tells his friend they'll be at the FBI headquarters in about 30 minutes.

When they pull up to the FBI building, Wayne's friend is waiting for him at the front door. He hands Wayne a sheet of paper.

"What's this?" Wayne asks.

"Thought you might want to look this over while we ride the elevator up to the lab," the FBI agent offers.

Before reading the document, Wayne introduces Mike to Special Agent Brad Haler. Wayne first met Special Agent Haler a few weeks after Wayne became head of the special task force to upgrade internal checks and balances of the protection branches of the government. This followed Wayne's discovery of their many weaknesses when he saved the President about a year ago. To perform the job, Wayne needed liaisons with all the branches—CIA, FBI, NSA, etc.—to coordinate a joint effort in the ongoing Homeland Security effort. Wayne's contact with the FBI is Brad, someone Wayne knows he can count on.

What Wayne reads sends shivers up his spine. The page is a breakdown of the man Wayne had asked for, a history of Garrett Coffman. Once you get past the basics—age, 45; birthplace, Detroit, Michigan; education, grade school (Field school in Park Ridge, Illinois), high school (Maine South in Park Ridge, Illinois), college (Carthage College in Kenosha, Wisconsin)—you see the heart of what Garrett Coffman really is, a trained killer. The picture attached is of a hardened face, with hazel eyes and dark brown hair.

Without a doubt, this is someone Wayne has heard about, not by name, but by reputation. After leaving Carthage College, Garrett Coffman joined the 75th Ranger Regiment, better known as the Army Rangers. He saw his first action in Operation Urgent Fury on Grenada in 1983. That's where he got his first taste of what he referred to as "necessary elimination." He then participated in Operation Just Cause in Panama in 1989 and again in the Gulf War's Desert Storm and Desert Shield in 1991. During the last two tours, his commander saw a talent that he passed on to his superiors. According to the report, "He has a unique ability to analyze a change in condition quickly, adapt to it, and execute the mission." This was a talent that the Central Intelligence Agency found important.

The report goes on to refer to him as "being considered as an eradicator," which Wayne knows is just a nicer way to say *assassin*. The report shows his being accepted and stipulates training requirements needed for his first assignment, though it does not talk of what the assignment was. The elevator bell sounds, informing the three men they have arrived at the floor housing the FBI lab. As they leave the elevator, Wayne tries to understand why a CIA assassin is heading an operation to retrieve the President's ledger.

Brad introduces Wayne and Mike to the lab technician, who is going to be analyzing the hard drives. "This is Ms. Lynn Ritt, our top analyst in data retrieval from damaged computer hard drives."

Lynn, a tall blonde-haired woman with model looks, gets up from behind her computer and holds out her hand, which Wayne grabs firmly and shakes, "If there is anything retrievable, I'll get it," Lynn tells Wayne and Mike with confidence.

They hand the computer hard drives to Lynn. Both Wayne and Mike understand this could take awhile, so they both decide it would be a good time to get something to eat. Wayne is especially hungry since he hasn't eaten a bite since breakfast yesterday. The technicians tell them they will call if they get anything. They take the elevator back down to the FBI cafeteria and get in line to pick out what they want from the food items under the glass.

After putting their selections on their trays, they pay and then move to a table near the back of the room so they can have some privacy. Wayne takes a moment before eating to finish reading the report on Garrett Coffman. Near the end of the report, it mentions the release of Coffman from the CIA to work as an "undercover consultant" for the Osburn administration. The report ends after that. *No wonder I never knew of him,* Wayne thinks. *He worked undercover.*

About 150 miles north, in a car speeding along Interstate 70 west, Taylor sits quietly in the back seat waiting until the guard next to her falls asleep so she can turn on her cell phone. She remembers Wayne telling her that just having a cell phone on makes it traceable.

The trip will take about 13 hours since it is over 800 miles to her college, the University of Wisconsin, so she knows the guard will doze off eventually. Fear keeps her awake. Taylor had decided on Wisconsin for two reasons: it's where her father went, and it has a reputation as a party school. She had been under Washington scrutiny so much during high school that she wanted to get a little wild during her college years.

As they continue on the drive to Wisconsin, Garrett questions Taylor further as to why she has the ledger. "So tell me, how is it you are in possession of your father's ledger?"

Taylor wonders what she should say. She knows she has to make sure he believes her. "When my dad died, I immediately flew home that night to be with my mom. That first night I sat at his desk, just exploring it to get close to him one more time. There was a loose panel next to the top left side drawer, and when I pushed it, it came out farther. There was a hollowed out section in the panel. I reached in and pulled out a small book filled with information, so I took it."

"And why did you do that?" Garrett pushes further.

"It had a lot of stuff in it, and I didn't want anyone else to see it," Taylor snaps back.

"What was in it?" Garrett continues his probing.

Taylor has to think quickly. "I really didn't examine it for fear my mom would see me with it, so I hid it and mailed it to my school address the next day."

"If my days are correct," Garrett adds to her statement, "that would mean you mailed it yesterday. If the mail system does its job, the package should get to your school by tomorrow. For yours and your mother's sake, pray the mail isn't delayed."

Garrett turns back around and stares out the front windshield while Mo continues to drive. He isn't completely sure of her story, but it does sound like she's seen it. His instinct tells him they are on the way to retrieving the ledger, so Garrett settles back in his seat and tries to catch some sleep.

Taylor, though, has even less chance of sleeping as she now worries about what happens after the delivery of her mail.

Seventeen

Optimistic

Wayne and Mike try to enjoy their meal, but events over the past hours have dulled their senses and left the taste of the food very bland. They are now just going through the motions of eating, taking their time and waiting for the results from the lab. Even small talk doesn't seem appropriate. Twenty minutes later, they finish pecking at their food as they sit back in their chairs and stare out at nothing in particular. A few minutes later, they decide to dispose of what is left of their food and head back up to the lab.

In the lab, Lynn still doesn't have anything definitive but is optimistic she can recover some of the memory from one of the hard drives and hopeful on a second. The two remaining hard drives have too much damage to retrieve anything recognizable. Lynn tells Wayne it might take a couple of more hours.

Brad suggests they both get some sleep and offers his office, which he claims has two nice couches. Both men agree that might help and walk down the hall to his office. Mike tells Wayne that Brad's word is gold as two comfortable couches framed his desk. Sleep doesn't come right away as they lay their heads down, but soon.

Back in the lab, Lynn continues to analyze the drives most capable of giving up any information. Putting the drives through a series of tests, she can tell if there is information on them and how it was filed. She then breaks down the information to see what form it takes, written, audio or video. Then with continual passes through a special computer with enhancing software, an image or sound will eventually start to emerge. It's a very time-consuming process, but if there is retrievable information, Lynn will find it.

It seemed like Wayne had just closed his eyes when he is brought back from what might have been a good dream, if he could remember it. "What, What?" Wayne calls out as coherently as possible in his groggy state.

"We have something for you," Brad excitedly informs him.

Wayne jumps up and shakes Mike awake. They then head up to the lab, where Lynn anxiously awaits their arrival. Entering the lab, Wayne walks to a chair in front of the computer where Lynn directs him to sit. Mike walks with Wayne and stands behind him.

"Lynn found many documents that refer to things I feel are government classified, but it's this video that we are most surprised with," Brad explains.

"We also discovered documents describing what happened before this video took place," Lynn says. "Things I don't believe anyone, anywhere is aware of."

Wayne's interest hits a new high as Lynn leans around him to press the enter key to start the video.

What comes up on the screen is a large group of people sitting in chairs in what looks like a cemetery. The camera angle is from the back so Wayne cannot tell who is there. It doesn't take long before the ceremony ends and the people in attendance start to get up and leave the service. He now can make out some of his contemporaries and former White House staff members. Many are crying and those not are very solemn and respectful of the occasion—all, that is, but one. Wayne cannot believe his eyes. It is past President Shane Osburn, walking and laughing. Wayne can tell from those attending the funeral service that he was not the past president then; he was the sitting president.

Walking with the president and laughing too is Agent Austin Ivers, who was the lead Secret Service Agent for Osburn during his presidency. Wayne now remembers this funeral; it is for John Blackard. John Blackard started with Shane Osburn on his election committee and was considered responsible for spearheading many initiatives that brought Osburn's campaign into public awareness. To reward him for all his help, Osburn appointed Blackard Secretary of Labor.

Things were on the fast track for John Blackard, but rumors started that he got the appointment to shut him up about something he supposedly knew about Osburn. Blackard always denied this whenever a reporter dared to question his credentials for the appointment. When he struggled with his job of handling labor unrest and was ineffective at mediating problems between the UAW and the automotive industry, there were calls for his removal. When talk started that Osburn was wavering on his support for Blackard, a newspaper reported that they would soon be breaking a story that will send shock waves through the administration.

About that time, Osburn sent Blackard on a trip to mediate a dispute between a packing plant and its 120 employees in little Lindsay, California. Osburn never fully explained to the media why such a trip was required. According to the plant executives and union, they were near an agreement already. In a backhanded remark a few weeks later, Osburn referred to the trip as a way to show his administration was not too big to react to even the smallest needs of the country.

Sadly, John Blackard never made it to the negotiations. His plane went down over the Colorado Rockies. It took four months before they could get to the wreck due to poor winter weather conditions that kicked up a day after the crash, along with the fact the plane's wreckage settled on a mountainside. Special high-altitude helicopters were required, but fear of the severe cold at that high altitude possibly freezing the engine required waiting for not only warmer weather, but also low winds, which are at their worst at that height.

When they finally reached the wreckage, it took specially trained military units to bring it down, along with the remains. The reports that came from the crash site brought cries of cover-up. At the time of the crash, local weather stations reported light snow, broken clouds at 400 feet, a thin overcast at 2000 feet, a steady head wind and visibility of five miles. Yet when the White House reported on the conditions during the crash, they said the plane flew into a freak snowstorm with blizzard winds, causing disorientation and a turn into the mountainside.

President Osburn's press secretary reported that the plane's cockpit carried neither voice recorder nor "black box," which, considering the First Lady had traveled on that same plane only a week earlier, brought many more questions. There also was no autopsy performed on any of the dead, including Blackard, even though those seeing the body noticed a perfectly round hole in the back of his head. That, the White House said, happened when a piece of metal hit Blackard as he "was thrown" from the cabin of the plane.

The White House arranged the funeral the day after Blackard's body arrived back in Washington. The same funeral Wayne is viewing right now. Running along the bottom of the video is a caption reading: "Osburn is pleased with the result." Near the end of the video, Osburn notices the video camera pointing at him and immediately changes from laughing to acting as if he is wiping tears from his eyes. Wayne shakes his head in disbelief and leans back in the chair as the video ends.

"If that shocks you," Brad hands Wayne a document, "this will knock you out."

Wayne takes the document, which contains five pages, and begins to look it over. In it are references to "being contacted" by a highly placed representative of "a potential employer" for "correcting a problem." It goes on to say that there was a meeting arranged with this representative and all "financial requirements were met" for the process to begin. Later in the document, it tells of surveillance starting concerning "the contract" and that "the contract is guaranteed to be on the plane."

The last couple of pages refer to the meetings with "the contract" and that the "required persuasion was effective." Listed at the end are a street address and two schools, a grade school and a high school, both in the Washington, D.C., area. An attached footnote reads, "It will be easy to locate other relatives if needed, but should not be necessary. As is standard policy, he was informed that an early end to him will not stop events for his family."

Wayne tries to absorb what he has read; it does not take much of a leap to understand that this document is a carefully worded order and handling of a blackmail plot, possibly ending in an assassination. However, as much as everything had an ominous sound to it, it never directly said anything or named anyone. The lack of names was very frustrating, but the date on the document was very telling: one month before John Blackard's plane crashed.

"Most everything else I was able to recover is of the same nature," Lynn informs Wayne, "but this document, along with the video, just stood out."

"You said 'most everything,'" Wayne points out. "Is there something else?"

"This," Lynn says as she hands Wayne another five-page document.

Wayne begins to read it over and immediately something stands out—the reference to a "prior employer's highly placed representative." Wayne continues to read and sees that the representative needs "the same action as done for him previously." It is pointed out further in the document that the "same guarantee cannot be in place" since the employer is "not in the same position to make such a guarantee." The same statements of "meeting the representative" and "financial requirements" locating "the contract" and "surveillance" are mentioned, along with the same ending footnote, except the address is different and there is only one school listed this time. The date on this document is almost to the day, one month ago. The same time allowed before Blackard's plane went down. Is this the same scenario, but now for the planning to down Air Force 2?

Austin Ivers' statement back at the Bender home now is coming in much clearer to Wayne: "We had to stop it" was what he said. It's now apparent to Wayne that the "representative" was Ivers. However, the statement just before that, "you can't threaten good people because things aren't going your way," now sounds like the epitome of audacity and the worst example of the pot calling the kettle black. Wayne cannot bring himself to consider whom Ivers was representing. Until there is undeniable proof, he has to remain loyal to the office. Wayne knows from years in Washington, that there are those that overstep their bounds under the pretense of doing what is right for their employer while the employer is out of the loop. His main job now is to get Taylor back safe. He'll save any judgment until that is accomplished.

"There is one more document you might want to look at," Lynn offers Wayne.

Wayne takes the one-page document to examine. At the top, it says in bold letters, "Rush Assignment" followed by "representative of previous employer states payment level is agreed to as long as contract can be completed within agreed-on date." It gives tomorrow as the needed completion date. Looking at his watch, Wayne sees it is nearly 6 a.m. The sun will be rising soon. Writing down the two addresses that were at the bottom of the first two documents, he hopes they will give him a lead to Taylor's location.

Wayne thanks Brad and Lynn for all their help and motions to Mike to follow him as he heads out of the lab and out of the FBI offices. Once in the car, Wayne types the first address into the car's GPS system and waits for the prompt as he drives out of the FBI parking lot.

Eighteen

Discovery

Taylor looks over at the guard who has been next to her continually since he roughly pushed her into the car, back in Dayton, Maryland. Amazingly, he has shown no sign of dozing off. Taylor knows she cannot risk turning her cell phone on for fear of discovery, but she also worries that the guard will soon notice he no longer has it in his pocket. She actually has nodded off but jerked awake by the loud snoring of the guy sitting in the front passenger seat. They now have been driving about four hours. Taylor can see the glow on the horizon, so it should not be too much longer before the sunrise. She bides her time for the right opportunity to turn on her cell phone.

Back in Washington, Wayne continues to follow the voice commands of the GPS system as it takes him and Mike across the city. During the trip, Mike questions Wayne about what he saw on the video and in the documents.

"The video looked bad," Mike starts, "with the President laughing like that at Blackard's funeral. I had heard other agents mention they had seen him do that. Were the documents you read tied to that plane crash?"

Wayne hesitates before answering, "Not in any way that could be used to arrest or convict, but they sure left me feeling I had read an agreement to end the life of a sitting cabinet member and all those on the plane with him."

Wayne decides not to discuss the other two documents since they were not part of the Blackard plane crash. For now, Wayne leaves it as just being about the Blackard crash. He hates that he is still concerned that Mike's loyalty is with Osburn, but until that changes, Wayne will keep much of what he knows to himself.

Mike, sensing he is still on the outside with Wayne, tries to offer some assurance, "Since being with Osburn, I've never been given the access to him that Ivers enjoyed. It was obvious they had a bond that I could not duplicate. It was never explained why he left Osburn to stay in Washington, but I know they stayed in touch. Periodically, Ivers would visit Osburn and any trip to Washington required a meeting with Ivers, which is why I had to meet with Ivers the other day, to set up the time for them to meet when Osburn came in for the funeral of Charles and Bender. Other than being part of Osburn's protection team, I have no ties to him."

Mike might not have realized it, but he further solidified the ties to Osburn and the deaths of Blackard and possibly Charles and Bender. If Austin Ivers was truly that close to Osburn, then the likelihood of Ivers dealing with Garrett Coffman on his own was remote. Wayne is still having trouble believing a sitting president could be a part of such a plot. *Then to continue this action against a sitting vice-president and chief of staff? Beyond imagination.*

The GPS is saying, "Make a turn left at the next street; then your destination is on the right."

Wayne makes the required turn and continues a few hundred feet. On the right, he can make out the street address he has written on the note pad. A moment later he pulls in front of the house. Wayne and Mike sit out in the car as Wayne stares at the house. This house looks eerily familiar to him. He continues to stare at it, hoping the memory will kick in, but nothing comes. Wayne looks at his watch to see that it is not quite 7 a.m., normally too early to ring the bell, but this is not a normal time. Wayne gets out of the car followed closely by Mike. As they reach the front door, Wayne can hear voices inside. He rings the bell.

Inside there's some commotion, and a male voice complains loudly, "Who would that be at this hour?"

The door opens and a man about 5 feet, 10 inches stands in front of Wayne and Mike. The face doesn't look familiar to Wayne, so he doesn't know why the house looks familiar.

"Can I help you?" the man asks, obviously annoyed.

Wayne holds out his Secret Service badge so the man can see it. "I'm Agent Wayne Mitchell and this is Agent Mike Peters. If you can spare a moment of your time, we need to ask you some questions."

The man's face goes from mad to concerned that he may be in trouble. "Yes, of course," the man quickly responds, "please come in."

He holds the door open for the two men so they can come into the house. Inside, Wayne sees a woman in the kitchen trying to get two children ready for school. The man walks the agents into the family room and offers them chairs. Once seated, Wayne knows he won't find Taylor or Garrett Coffman here, but he needs to ask some questions anyway.

"We are investigating the disappearance of a couple of people, and this address was found on a document that might be tied to someone that had something to do with it."

The man looks shocked at this revelation. "I'm sorry that someone has disappeared, but I cannot imagine why our house was listed in any way."

"How long have you lived here?" Wayne questions.

"We bought the house six years ago."

"Do you remember who you bought it from?" Wayne responds.

"I think the name was Spain, yes, Spain. I remember because of the uniqueness of it. I had never heard a country as a sir name before."

Why does that name mean something? Wayne thinks for a minute, then it dawns on him why the house looks so familiar. It was on the news following the Blackard plane crash. This was the home of pilot Steve Spain. He flew the doomed plane. Spain must be the person referred to as "the contract." Wayne goes over in his mind what all was mentioned in the document and remembers phrases: "required persuasion" and that they could "locate other relatives if needed."

Overcome by what he now has to believe, Wayne has trouble contemplating what must have happened. Coffman, or someone that works for him, must have contacted Spain to threaten his family's safety to force him to do something no one would conceivably do: deliberately crash the plane.

Wayne abruptly stands and thanks the man for his help. Mike also stands as he follows Wayne to the front door. They let themselves out, then walk to their car. Wayne sits behind the steering wheel and stares out through the windshield at nothing in particular, trying to put what he now believes into perspective. Who could guarantee that a certain pilot will fly a certain plane? He may not have personally assigned Spain, but whoever did it knew the instructions came from someone of unquestionable authority.

Mike is beside himself wondering what just happened inside the house. "What are you thinking, Wayne?"

Wayne looks over at Mike. "I can't really say yet."

The car carrying Taylor continues to make its way to the University of Wisconsin as she looks up from another moment of near sleep, disturbed again by the loud snoring from the front passenger seat. With her eyes still a little blurred from the little sleep she got, she can see in the distance a rest stop sign.

"I need to use a bathroom," Taylor announces, realizing a stop at the rest area will be the opportunity she has been waiting for.

Hearing Taylor's need for relief, Garrett Coffman awakes from the front seat and acknowledges his need for a bathroom break too. Mo Mower points to the approaching sign and its reference to a rest stop in two miles. The men agree to get off the highway and use the facility. A couple of minutes later the car comes to a stop amongst the cars of others wanting to use the facility. Garrett knows he has to be careful on what he allows Taylor to do and he has a way to handle it.

"Do not talk to anyone while we are here," Garrett instructs her. "If you do, they will die, do you understand?"

Taylor nods. They then all exit the car. As the four of them enter the building, Garrett looks for the security officer and approaches him. "Officer, I'm with the Secret Service."

Taylor sees Coffman pull out a badge and show it to the officer.

"We are the security team protecting this young lady. She needs to use the bathroom, but we will require it be empty before she can enter it."

The officer understands and walks over to the women's washroom and calls into it to see if anyone is there. One voice calls out that she is there but will be out in a minute. Soon a middle-aged woman exits the bathroom and the officer motions the men that it is now safe to let the young woman use the bathroom. Coffman has Taylor's guard bring her to the bathroom entrance, then lets her enter on her own.

Taylor walks in and goes to the last stall. Closing the door behind her, she pulls the cell phone from the front pocket of her jeans where she had been able to tuck it just after taking it from the guard. Opening it, she pushes the power button and watches as the screen goes through its start-up sequence before settling on the picture she had designated as her background image, a picture of her dad in the Oval Office with the President.

She looks to see if any bars are showing the strength of the signal and sees three. She puts the phone in her pocket, then uses the facility since she really did have to. As she goes to the other side of the bathroom to wash her hands and fix her hair, she can hear her captors talking. The boss is questioning the one who is driving about how he figures their office was located.

"How could they have known where we were?" Coffman challenges Mower.

"I know we took the phone from the daughter," Mower replies, "but maybe the mother really did have her phone and was able to hide it."

"I know. I should have allowed the cavity search," Coffman concedes.

Just then Taylor hears her guard come back from using the men's washroom.

"You still have the girl's cell phone, don't you?" Coffman questions the guard as he gets next to the other two men.

"Yes, of course, sir," the man responds confidently, then reaches into his right front pocket. Not finding it there, he reaches into his left front pocket. He begins to panic as he searches his rear two pockets to no avail.

"Oh, no," Coffman responds, immediately suspecting the daughter has it. Coffman quickly enters the women's bathroom. In the background there's the faint sound of a toilet flushing. Startled by the entrance of a man in this sacred room for women, Taylor leans back against the sink in fear as he charges toward her.

"Okay, where is it?" Coffman firmly asks.

"Where is what?" Taylor meekly responds.

Coffman doesn't waste time discussing it further. He grabs her by the shoulders and turns her until she is facing away from him, then starts patting her down along her sides and back.

"What are you doing?" Taylor responds more assertively.

Coffman turns her around to face him again. "Unless you want me to start searching your front, you had better give up that cell phone," he demands.

"You took my cell phone when you kidnapped my mother and me," Taylor reminds him. "Your guard has my cell phone."

"He should have it, but somehow he doesn't," Coffman reluctantly admits. "I'd like to give you the benefit of the doubt, but I can't. I can physically search you, or you can remove your clothes."

Taylor, shocked at the choice, doesn't answer him.

"Come on. I don't have all day. How do you want to do this?" Coffman prods impatiently.

Taylor doesn't want this man touching her further, but she surely doesn't want to remove her clothes for him. "Go ahead and search me." Taylor resigns herself to her fate and holds her arms out for his inspection.

Coffman quickly searches her, making sure not to allow for any hiding place for the phone. Once satisfied she doesn't have it on her, he moves about the bathroom. He goes into each stall, checking the bowls and water tanks. Lastly, he looks inside the wastebasket but doesn't find the phone there either. Coffman looks at Taylor to try to see if anything in her expression would say that she has the phone somewhere, but all he sees is a young girl who was originally scared, but is now mad.

"I'm sorry." Coffman abruptly apologizes for what he did and then leaves to allow her to finish what she was doing.

Taylor leans against the sink, takes a deep breath, and lets it out slowly. She knows how lucky she was that she had overheard their conversation. She could tell that they were aware she might have the phone. She just barely had time to drop it in the toilet bowl and flush it.

She can only hope that Wayne was looking for the phone signal and caught it before it went down the toilet. Outside the bathroom, Taylor can hear the boss chastising her guard for losing the phone. They eventually decide it must have come out of his pocket during the escape from Dayton. A minute later Taylor comes out of the washroom and the four of them head back to the car.

Nineteen

Suspicions

Wayne considers his options as he pulls out of the driveway. He decides to call Brad at the FBI again to confirm his suspicions that the home address of the pilot of Air Force 2 matches the address at the bottom of the second document. As he reaches for the phone, it begins to ring. He looks at the name at the bottom of the screen and sees it's Brad.

"Hello," Wayne answers his phone.

"Wayne, this is Brad. Thought you might want to know, the cell phone that went active last night went active again a few minutes ago."

"Man, that's great news. Did you get a location?"

"Yes, we were lucky, because it went dead after only a couple of minutes. It's about five hours north on Interstate 70 west, just past Pennsylvania and Ohio Stateline. On the map it looks like it could be a rest area just past Hendrysburg, Ohio."

"Thanks for keeping vigilance on it. I need one more thing."

"Sure, Wayne."

"The address on that second document Lynn showed me…could you check to see if you can find the name it is listed under?"

"It shouldn't take more than a few minutes. Do you want to hold?"

"Yes, I'll hold."

Wayne heads the car toward Interstate 270, which will intersect with Interstate 70 about 30 miles north. He picks up speed when he can, but until he gets to the expressway, he won't be making any time gains. A few minutes later Brad is back on the phone.

"Wayne, the name is Ingrid Fisher."

A long pause is held by both ends of the phone before Brad continues, "You know who that is, don't you?" Brad says in a knowing tone, aware who Ingrid Fisher is, or in this case *was*.

"Yes." Wayne confirms Brad's suspicion, but the name is not exactly the one Wayne thought he would hear. He had expected to hear the name Chris Hogh, who was captain of Air Force 2 the night it went down. Instead, he hears the co-captain's name. Maybe Coffman was unable to make contact with Hogh, or more likely, he felt he would have more success threatening the children of a female pilot. Either way they were successful in crashing Air Force 2, leaving no survivors.

"Brad," Wayne continues, "I'm going to leave my cell phone on so you can trace me. As we approach the location you saw, call me."

"Sure will, Wayne. I'll talk to you again in a few hours."

Wayne hangs up and puts his phone back in his pocket as he continues to drive. Mike looks over at Wayne, wondering if he should say something to break the silence. He is concerned that Wayne still doesn't trust him enough to take him into his confidence. Mike knows if he is truly going to help, it will be best to know Wayne has his back and that he has Wayne's.

"Wayne," Mike begins, "was the name Brad gave you a lead?"

Wayne looks over at Mike briefly, then turns his head back to the road. "In a way. It mostly confirmed a suspicion."

"And what is that?" Mike prods.

Wayne again turns his head to Mike, but this time he gives him an icy stare before looking back at the road. Mike has no problem picking up that Wayne has decided to keep that to himself, but Mike isn't so inclined to allow it.

"Look, Wayne, I don't know what else I can do to convince you that I'm with you 100 percent. I've even left my dead brother to help you. What more do you want?"

Wayne looks back at Mike, but this time with a little softer stare. Turning back to the road, he begins to tell him some of what he knows as he directs the car off Interstate 270 and onto Interstate 70 west. He begins by telling Mike that the President asked him to retrieve the same ledger Tim had mentioned he was unable to find in Bender's office.

"I went to the Bender estate to ask his wife and daughter if they knew of it. While I was there, a black car with some men pulled up and before I knew it, more men had surrounded the house and I was in the middle of protecting the Bender women while still trying to locate the ledger. After being able to repel numerous attempts to enter the house, they sent in someone I thought was a friend, Austin Ivers. It didn't take long to see he was no friend. I was able to get the advantage and use him to get us out of the house. They killed him not long after that to keep him quiet."

"I took the women to what I hoped was a safe spot, so not to risk their lives further, but it turned out it wasn't safe, and they were gone when I returned. That's when I questioned your brother, then you, in hopes to get a lead as to who had Kathy and Taylor. That brings you up to speed. We now have Kathy safe and know Coffman has Taylor. We just don't know where yet, but we will."

"Would knowing what's in the ledger help?" Mike asks.

"Why, do you know what is in it?" Wayne challenges Mike.

"No, I thought maybe you knew," Mike responds defensively.

"The President will decide who he wants to know," Wayne states firmly.

"Yes, of course. I just thought it might help," Mike adds.

Wayne has to admit he cannot find fault with Mike's reasoning. Obviously, a name on the list is why all this has happened and the time to question the President more may be soon.

A few minutes pass without any more conversation until Mike asks, "What was the significance of the two addresses?"

Now Wayne has to decide if he's going to bring Mike into his trust concerning the evidence that is building against former president Shane Osburn. If he does, will Mike be defensive and possibly further hurt their ability to trust each other, or will he be receptive to the facts and see how they point in the direction of the ex-president?

"Mike," Wayne begins, "I'm about to tell you some things that might affect our future relationship. Are you sure you want to hear?"

Mike quickly responds, "If I'm going to be able to effectively help you and President Anders, I need to know."

Wayne begins, "One of the people involved is Garrett Coffman, whom you overheard Osburn talking about to Ivers a month ago. Brad gave me a breakdown on him when we were at the FBI. He's a U.S. government-trained assassin who worked for the CIA before transferring to the Osburn administration to be an undercover consultant. Obviously, after leaving Osburn, he started his own business. That was his building that held Kathy and Taylor. Those were his hard drives we took to the FBI for analysis. Now, what was on those hard drives is the kicker. You saw the video that was taken of Osburn and Ivers laughing as they left the funeral of Secretary Blackard, but you didn't see the documents written and dated a month before that video. Those documents detail a precise plan to eliminate someone and the person that will carry out the elimination. The address we went to used to be the home of Steve Spain. Does that name mean anything to you?"

Mike shakes his head. "No, but I have a strong feeling it has to do with that video."

"Steve Spain," Wayne explains, "was the pilot of the plane that crashed killing Secretary Blackard. At that time, a rumor said that Blackard had shocking information about Osburn and that he had agreed to talk to a reporter soon. The documents referred to 'a contract,' and I believe that was a reference to Steve Spain. I first thought 'the contract' referred to the one to die, but after the visit to the home, it is now obvious that 'the contract' refers to who was going to do the killing. Coffman picked, or had picked for him, a person to persuade through extraordinary means, to perform the ultimate assassination, one that would kill the assassin too. The only sure way to convince a person to do the unimaginable is to threaten that person's family. The documents say that other relatives are available if needed and that if 'the contract' kills himself before accomplishing his directive, his family would die anyway. Here is a man faced with his family's death if he does not crash the plane, killing everyone in it. What would you do, Mike?"

Mike shakes his head, unable to say, but worries that deep down he too would have crashed the plane.

"The next address was attached to the second document and laid out the same scenario as the first, only it was dated about a month ago. This time though, 'the contract' did not refer to the pilot, but instead to the co-pilot. Would you venture to guess what plane this person was the co-pilot of?"

Mike, using the same timeline of one month before the actual crash, hesitantly says, "Air Force 2."

"Ingrid Fisher had to listen to how her children would die if she refused to crash that plane, killing not only the chief of staff, but also the Vice-President of the United States. Truthfully, I do not know if I would have done anything different from co-pilot Fisher. It is one thing to protect who you are assigned to, but if it meant my family would die instead, I just don't know if I could allow them to die."

Mike, listening intently, picks up on the co-pilot's name. "You said the co-pilot was Fisher?"

"Yes," Wayne replies.

"Ingrid Fisher?" Mike further questions.

"Yes," Wayne answers with a lot more interest in the question.

Mike thinks back to that conversation he walked in on a month ago. This is all too unbelievable, but Mike knows now what he has to do. "Wayne, that conversation a month ago, when I overheard Osburn and Ivers mention Coffman...well, just before that they said the name *Fisher*. To be exact, they said, 'Have Coffman contact Ingrid Fisher; she will be on it.'"

Wayne realizes he has just received the final piece to the puzzle.

Nearly 300 miles away, Taylor continues to look out the window of the car as it quickly passes through the city of Columbus, Ohio. She had never really wanted to visit there before, but now she wishes she had that option. The men in the car with her are thankfully not talkative, so she can at least pass the time her own way, by staring out the side window and praying. She prays her mother is safe and that Wayne was able to pick up her cell phone signal before she flushed it down the toilet. But mostly she prays that God will watch over her.

Twenty

Drive

Wayne notices they are just about to enter the state of Ohio from Pennsylvania. It shouldn't be too much longer before they reach where the last cell phone activity came from. Wayne and Mike now both agree that a past president played some part in two planes crashing and probably gave the directive to recover "the list" that Bender and President Anders kept. That he allowed a monster of a human being to threaten the lives of someone's family in order to eliminate a political problem is unbelievable to them both. Somehow, the two of them will find a way to bring justice to those responsible.

They have been driving for about 5 hours and Wayne knows that Coffman and Taylor are at least that much ahead of them. He wonders where they could be going. After about ten minutes of additional driving, Wayne's phone rings. It is Brad, telling them that they should be coming up on where the last cell phone activity was. Brad stays on the line as Wayne continues west on Interstate 70. A couple of minutes pass before Wayne can see a dark green sign about a mile ahead. As they approach, Wayne is able to make out the words REST AREA ONE MILE.

"Brad, a rest area is just ahead. Stay on the line, though, just in case," Wayne instructs.

"Sure thing, I'm here if you need me."

Wayne makes the turn off the expressway onto the entrance ramp of the rest area. Seconds later, they park and enter the building. Once inside Wayne looks around the large open reception area. He then sees a security officer standing off a ways. Wayne quickly approaches him.

"Hello, Officer," Wayne says as he brings out his identification, "I was wondering if you might have noticed a young girl, long blond hair, blue eyes, very pretty?"

"Yes, I do remember her," the officer states. "She was with some of your other agents."

Wayne at first is taken aback by that statement, then recovers. "Did one of those other agents have dark brown hair? Was he about my height?"

"Yes, I believe so."

"How many agents were there?"

"I only saw three, but more could have been outside. I'm sorry; I really didn't pay that much attention. They came in, used the bathrooms, and left."

"How long ago was that?"

"Gosh, I'd say around 5 or 6 hours ago. It was very early in the morning, so probably just after 6 a.m. It wasn't much past that because the morning sun was glaring through the window over there when they came in." The officer points to the east side of the building.

"Did you notice anything out of the ordinary?"

"Well, there was that time the man you described went into the ladies' washroom for awhile, but I took it that the lady had called for him. He came out and she followed soon after."

Wayne looks at his watch and sees it is just past 11:30 a.m. Both men quickly use the washroom, then get back into the car. Wayne tells Brad to continue to monitor the cell phone calls and to let him know if he hears anything. Brad confirms this and hangs up. Wayne has to make one more call.

"White House, can I help you?" the White House operator says.

"Yes, this is Agent Mitchell; can you put me through to the private quarters?"

"Of course, Agent Mitchell. Right away."

The phone rings a couple of times before being picked up, "First Family's quarters, this is Agent Yeater."

"Hi Reed, this is Wayne Mitchell. Is Kathy Bender there?"

"Yes, Wayne, I'll get her."

Agent Reed Yeater is First Lady Claire Anders' lead agent. Claire is obviously staying with Kathy during this trying time. A few moments pass before Kathy picks up the phone.

"Wayne," Kathy anxiously answers the phone, "have you found her?"

"Not yet Kathy, but I know she is alive." Wayne can hear Kathy sigh with relief on the other end. "We just talked with someone who saw her about 5 hours ago. We are on Interstate 70 heading west; would you know if she is taking them somewhere that would be along this way?"

There is silence on the other end as Kathy tries to think, but she cannot come up with anything. Wayne can then hear her ask for a roadmap. Kathy tells Wayne to hold on for a second as she gets a map. Soon Wayne can hear Kathy say, "Thank you," followed by the sound of paper rustling.

"I got it," Kathy exclaims excitedly. "I think she is taking them to her college, the University of Wisconsin." Kathy waits a few seconds, then asks, "That is the way her father and I took her that first year, but why would she be going there?"

"She's scared," Wayne, replies. "If what you said is true, she may have convinced them she has what they want at her college to give her and us more time. We were able to trace her here through her phone, but it is not on anymore. If the University of Wisconsin is their destination, do you have her roommate's name?"

Kathy thinks for a moment. "Yes, it's Deb, Debbie Lawrence."

"Would you happen to know what she looks like?" Wayne inquires.

"She's a brunette, about 5 feet, 6 inches, very pretty with a nice figure."

"Thanks. Don't worry, we'll get Taylor back." Wayne says goodbye to Kathy and puts the phone away as he pushes down on the car's accelerator. Soon the car's speedometer is touching 80 mph as he tries to keep an eye out for any highway patrols that might pop up.

About 5 hours further west, Taylor continues to look out the side window of the car. She notices they are now on Interstate 74 west after passing through Indianapolis. They had just stopped again to use the restroom at a gas station while they filled the car with gas. She had hoped to get someone's attention, but everyone there just went about their own business. Her personal guard never let her out of his sight, except during her time in the bathroom. Again, the men made sure it was empty before allowing her to enter, and they guarded the entrance until she came out.

She took as long in the washroom as she deemed safe, afraid one of the men might burst in on her again, and then was hustled back into the car once she came out. The other two men picked up some snacks and drinks and offered a choice to Taylor. She picked out a turkey and cheese sandwich and a diet Pepsi, then settled back in her seat as they pulled away from the gas station. The man driving turned on the radio and some country music starts playing.

"Now that is my kind of music," the driver says.

The guard next to Taylor smiles but does not say anything, nor does the front seat passenger. Taylor goes back to her thoughts of her dad and her mom and the hope that Wayne will find her as she sits and prays in silence.

Back on Interstate 70, Wayne has pushed the car's speed to 90 mph. He has to narrow the time gap between him and Coffman, so the risk is acceptable. Wayne senses that Coffman will not risk getting a ticket, so if he can maintain about a 20 mph difference, he can reduce their time advantage by more than a couple of hours by the time he gets to Wisconsin. They picked up some food and beverages at the rest stop, so they can eat and drive. If all goes according to plan, they should reach Madison, Wisconsin, in about 7 hours, maybe less. That would put them at the university by about 6 p.m. Central time. Considering

Coffman's lead and driving not much over the speed limit, Wayne figures that they will be there by about 4 p.m. Central time.

Wayne calls Brad back. "Would you be able to contact your office in Milwaukee and see if they could send some agents to the University of Wisconsin campus?"

"I guess," Brad responds, sounding a little puzzled. "What do you have in mind?"

"I think Coffman is heading there. I need you to e-mail that picture of Garrett Coffman to your office there and have your people position themselves in key locations around the main campus. Especially have someone keep an eye on Taylor's roommate, Debbie Lawrence."

Wayne passes on Debbie's description to Brad before explaining more. "You can contact the registrar's office to see what dorm she is in. I estimate Coffman's arrival to be about 4 p.m. Central time, so you have less than 4 hours to get your people there and in place. You might also want to e-mail my picture to them so they know who I am. And Brad, make sure they stay invisible."

"I'm on it, Wayne. Call me when you get there and I'll have the agents contact you." Brad hangs up so he can start making arrangements as Wayne passes some slower driving cars. It's now just a matter of time.

Wayne looks over at Mike and is glad he has him along. In the last few hours, Wayne's trust of him has grown. That's an important thing between agents, trust. With that, you know when you go into any situation your back is covered. Wayne looks back at the road, makes his way around more cars as he continues to push it over 90 mph.

Ahead, in Garrett Coffman's car, they are cruising along at just over the speed limit. Fast enough to be making decent time, but not fast enough to call attention to them. Since passing Indianapolis, they have traveled another 3 hours, passing through Bloomington, Illinois, and onto Interstate 39 north, which will take them to Madison, Wisconsin. Since they should get to the campus by 4 p.m., Garrett's plan is for them to head to the student union, where, according to Taylor, the students pick up their mail. Garrett does not have great hope that the ledger will be there yet, but there is no harm in checking, just in case the mail happened to have had a good couple of travel days.

Taylor, seeing they are getting within a few hours of the campus, requests another bathroom stop. Garrett allows it but tells her it's the last one until they reach her school. The car turns off at the next exit in search of another gas station. A couple of miles off the highway they pull into a Fast 'N' Go. The guard follows Taylor to the bathroom and makes sure no one is in it before letting her enter, while the other two men use the facility and fill up the car again with gas.

Taylor once again takes as much time as possible in the bathroom, but soon the guard yells for her to hurry up. Taylor yells back that she will be out in a minute, then waits next to the door, stalling. She figures that when he gets annoyed enough to try to enter, she will pretend she is just walking out. In a couple more minutes she hears him turning the door handle. As the door opens, Taylor is right there at the entrance and walks past him to the car. The guard shakes his head in frustration, follows her to the car, then goes back to use the men's bathroom. A few minutes later, all are back in the car and returning to the expressway.

At just before 4 p.m., they are on the outskirts of the campus of the University of Wisconsin. Garrett has Taylor give Mo directions to the student union. As they travel along the streets of the large campus, Taylor periodically sees a familiar face and wishes there was some way to communicate to them, but then remembers the threat of their death if she does. A sudden fear races through her as she wonders what will happen if someone recognizes her. Softly she begins to cry.

Twenty-one

Precautions

Taylor points out the student union to the men as the car drives past an impressive open area surrounded by large academic buildings. Turning the car toward where Taylor pointed, Garrett can see that the student union is a large building, almost rustic looking, nestled amongst trees, overlooking Lake Mendota. In a way, it fits the rest of the campus, which is a mixture of old and new. About a mile to the right, blocked by a row of school buildings, is the state capitol building.

Mo finds a parking space near the front of the student union parking lot. Garrett looks around the area for anything out of place. He will keep Taylor very close to him. He doesn't think anyone knows where they are, but he's not so stupid as to forget to take precautions. In his business, precautions are an everyday necessity. He gets out of the car and opens Taylor's door for her. She hesitates, but sees the man's frustration so she slowly swings her legs out of the door and gets out of the car. Mo and the guard also get out and wait for Garrett and Taylor to lead the way.

Garrett holds Taylor by the right elbow and whispers to her a little reminder, "If I see you try to communicate to anyone about what we are here for, that person will die. Do you understand me?"

"Yes," Taylor softly responds.

"Okay then, lead the way," Garrett tells her while giving her a mild tug on the elbow.

Taylor starts walking toward the entrance of the student union, all the while hoping not to see anyone she recognizes or who recognizes her. Entering the building, Taylor looks up at the clock that hangs in the entrance hall and smiles. *4:04 p.m.* She's done all she can to stall for time.

Garrett continually scans the area for any sign of a problem as he hangs onto Taylor's elbow. He jerks to the right when he hears a voice call out, "Taylor."

Taylor looks to her right and sees a classmate.

"Hey," the friend calls out, "so sorry about your dad."

"Thank you," Taylor responds curtly and keeps walking.

The friend looks puzzled as he watches Taylor walk away, wondering if he did something to make her mad and why she would be back at school when her dad's funeral is in a couple of days. He shrugs his shoulders and accepts that Taylor must have her reasons.

Taylor continues to make her way through the building with the three men following closely.

Outside, a local FBI agent makes a call to Brad Haler at FBI headquarters in Washington to tell him that they have seen Coffman. Brad gives the agent Wayne's cell phone number and instructs him to inform Wayne and to take directions from him now. The agent calls Wayne next and informs him of the sighting.

"Thanks. How many agents do you have on the campus?" Wayne asks.

"Three," replies the agent.

"Leave one with the roommate, Debbie Lawrence. You and the second agent monitor Coffman. Do not lose him," Wayne instructs. "I should be on campus in about two hours. I'll call you when I'm there."

The agent hangs up, then contacts the second agent to meet him at the student union.

Inside the building, Taylor has arrived at the mailroom with the other three men, but, as she hoped, the mailroom closed at 4 p.m. She locates her mailbox, which is on the outside wall of the mailroom, but informs the men that she cannot get into it.

"Why not?" Garrett challenges her.

"If you remember, you took me and my mom so quickly from the park police station that we left our purses. My mailbox key is in my purse," Taylor answers a little sarcastically.

"So how do you plan to get into it?" Garrett inquires firmly.

"It's too late today. The mailroom people have all left. But tomorrow I can have one of them open it for me," Taylor explains.

"And when do the mailroom people arrive?" Garrett asks impatiently.

"I think it's 9 a.m.," Taylor answers.

Garrett accepts the answer but that doesn't keep him from getting mad. He turns to Mo Mower and snarls at him to locate a place they can stay the night. Mo walks over to a phone booth at the far end of the hall and rifles through the phonebook that hangs from a chain next to it. Garrett grabs Taylor's elbow again and directs her to start walking back to the car.

From a corner of one of the academic buildings lining the mall that fronts the student union, an FBI agent watches the entrance to the building intently. Soon he sees Coffman leaving the student union with a young woman and another man in tow. Concerned where the third man is, the FBI agent radios to his other agent at the back of the building to keep watch for an older man leaving from the back. A couple of minutes later the third man appears outside the student union, heading toward the other three.

Mo gets into the driver's side of the car. "I contacted one of our people out of Milwaukee and he is letting us use his place in Lake Mills, about 30 minutes east of here."

"Good, we can get back here first thing in the morning. Let's get out of here," Coffman tells Mo, who starts the car and pulls out of the parking lot.

The FBI agent watching contacts his other agent to meet him at the car. He then calls the agent watching the roommate to tell him to stay near her while they follow the subject. Neither agent runs to their car, not wanting to draw attention, but also there is no reason since they attached a homing device to the bottom of the subject's car while they were inside the student union. A few minutes more and they are on the road, following the homing signal. While driving, the agent calls Wayne to tell him what has happened and what they are doing.

"I'm just over an hour away," Wayne states, "so keep me posted on your location so I can follow you."

The agent agrees and hangs up. He maintains a safe distance behind the trace vehicle so as not to give even the slightest opportunity for detection. The homing device will do all the work. They leave Madison on US 151 north, then turn onto Interstate 94 east. Watching the tracking monitor, the agent can see the subject is traveling at 66 mph so the agent maintains that speed. After about 20 minutes, the monitor indicates the subject is turning off the highway about a mile from where the agents are. The GPS shows that to be the town of Lake Mills.

Six minutes later, following the homing signal, the agents turn off the expressway onto route 89 south, into Lake Mills. About a quarter mile off 94, the subject car turns west on Tyranena Park Road. One half mile later they turn south onto West Madison Street, then a few blocks later turn west onto Shore Acres Road. The agents hang back on West Madison Street until they get a better feel for where the subject car ends up. It doesn't take long before they see that it has stopped at the end of Shore Acres Road. The agents park and travel the rest of the way on foot, hiding amongst the trees and homes until they see the subject car parking in the driveway of the last house on the road.

Mo pulls the car into the driveway of what looks like a very nice home on Rock Lake. Garrett has Mo look the place over before the rest get out. After checking the front, Mo goes around back and, seeing everything is fine, locates the key that the owner said would be under a plank of the boat dock. He then comes back around front to let everyone in.

It's not surprising that Garrett Coffman's employees have such nice homes. He has always paid well to those who do what he asks of them. The clients pay substantial sums for the services that Coffman provides, and he passes on a fair percentage to his employees located across the United States and various spots throughout the world.

Upon entering the house, Mo walks over to the security pad that has been giving off a high-pitched sound since they came in and punches in the deactivation code that the owner gave him. Garrett tells Taylor's guard to stay with her as he and Mo look around the house to make sure everything is okay. A few minutes later, they are all back together and ordering pizza.

Back down on West Madison Street, the agents have returned to their car to wait. They have already called Wayne and told him their location and were told to wait for his arrival. Wayne figured it would take about 45 minutes for him to get there. The agents watch Shore Acres Road to make sure the subjects do not leave. While they wait for Wayne, the sun begins to set.

At about the 45-minute mark, the agents see a car's headlights turn onto West Madison Street from Tyranena Park Road. Seconds later the car's headlights flash to signal who they are. The agents exit their car as Wayne's vehicle pulls up next to them. Wayne rolls down the window of his car.

"I'm Agent Wayne Mitchell and this is Agent Mike Peters. Any activity?"

The FBI agents introduce themselves. "I'm Special Agent Fred

Grafton, and this is Special Agent Larry Kotewa. Special Agent Mike Leali is guarding the roommate. We haven't seen anything since they went in. They are in the last house on Shore Acres Road," the FBI agent answers.

Just then, another pair of headlights turns onto West Madison Street from Tyranena Park Road. The agents quickly turn toward their parked car as Wayne pulls his car in front. Trying to act as if they belong, the agents casually get back into their car. The new pair of headlights continues to approach toward the agents until reaching the intersection of Shore Acres Road, then turns. When the car is out of sight, the four men get out of their cars and follow on foot through the trees and homes along Shore Acres Road.

Once within viewing range, they can see the car pull into the same driveway that the subjects pulled into. Wayne peers around the tree he is at and focuses his attention on who leaves the car. A second later, a person carries something to the front door. It's too dark to make out who he is or what he is carrying. All of a sudden the front porch light turns on and Wayne smiles. A pizza deliveryman. The front door then opens and out steps Mo Mower to pay for the pizza. He hands over the money, grabs the two boxes, and disappears behind the door.

After the pizza man leaves, Wayne signals the other agents over to him, "Do we know now many are in the house?"

"No, but three men and a woman entered," Agent Grafton, answers.

Wayne nods. "The woman is a hostage, so make sure nothing happens to her. I'm going over to the house to try to find a way in. I'll be back in a minute."

Wayne stealthily makes his way down the street to the house. He then moves around the bushes of the house, trying not to be seen while he checks on ways to possibly enter. In the back of the house, the land falls away and reveals a door to the basement. Wayne tries to turn the handle, but no luck. A window is on each side of the door. Wayne tries them both, but with the same result. He sees where the electric meter and power line come into the house. There is a deck above him so he walks up the deck stairs as quietly as he can. At the top of the stairs, he can see a large sliding-glass door that opens from the house onto the large wood deck. It is open, allowing the refreshing night air into the house.

Looking inside the house toward the kitchen, he sees Taylor standing stiffly as three men hover around the pizza that has just arrived. He now recognizes Garrett Coffman. He stands next to Taylor and hands her a plate for her to use for her meal. She accepts it from him but makes no move to take any pizza. Mo Mower hands some beers from the refrigerator to another man, takes some pizza, and moves out of sight. Wayne watches a few seconds longer before he carefully takes the stairs down and works his way back to his men.

Twenty-two

Lethal Force

His men are noticeably anxious when Wayne returns to explain what he saw, "They are in the back of the house eating. I believe there are only the three men with the hostage. They have left the sliding glass doors open off the upper deck. My car has what we need." Wayne refers to the equipment that he, Tim, and Mike had loaded up late yesterday when they went to Coffman's place in Dayton, Maryland. At Wayne's car, the four men grab the assault rifles, knives, teargas canisters, oxygen cylinders and night-vision goggles Wayne has in the trunk of the car. Wayne also has Mike grab the cable cutters to cut the power.

Wayne begins to lay out his plan. "Mike and I will make our way around back. Fred, you and Larry maintain a position at the front of the house, preventing any exit. Try not to use lethal force, but do not hesitate if required to save the hostage or yourselves."

Fred and Larry nod.

"Okay, let's go." Wayne turns and leads them down Shore Acres Road to the house.

At the house, they separate with Mike and Wayne moving quietly in the growing darkness to the back. Wayne shows Mike the power line and tells him to stay and cut the power when he signals. Wayne then slowly takes the steps up to the deck. At a couple of steps from the top of the stairs, Wayne stops and slowly raises his head to peer over the floor of the deck. The sliding doors are still open and at that moment, he hears the distinct voice of Mo Mower telling someone to turn the channel on the TV. Wayne then sees Mo coming to the sliding doors and pushes aside the screen door so he can come out on the deck.

Wayne hand motions Mike to stay very still as they hear Mo walk out onto the deck. Wayne and Mike listen to his footsteps walk to the end of the deck where he leans against the railing, drinking one of the beers he took from the refrigerator. Inside the house is the sound of a television show, then the changing of the channel, until finally settling on what sounds like a comedy show.

"Hey Mo!" yells the man's voice from inside, "I found a Seinfeld rerun."

Mo gives a short laugh before stepping away from the railing and back into the house. Wayne hears the screen door close behind him. He waits a few seconds then peers back over the deck floor again. He sees Coffman briefly walk across the room to the kitchen, open the refrigerator, and grab a beer before going out of sight again. Wayne makes his way to the top step and crawls on his belly along the deck.

It is only about 15 feet from the steps to the sliding glass doors, but on your belly, it seems a lot farther. Just before reaching the door, Wayne reaches for his knife and one of the teargas canisters. He then squirms the last foot to the screen door. The television is just loud enough to cover the slight sound of Wayne cutting the bottom of the screen. He motions to Mike through the opening between the planks of the deck to cut the power in 10 seconds. At 8 seconds, he puts the oxygen cylinder in his mouth, pulls the tab of the teargas canister while pushing up the cut screen, then throws the canister through the opening in the screen just before it explodes. In one motion, Wayne jumps to a standing position while putting on his night-vision goggles, then dives through the screen door as the lights go out.

Reaching around his back, he brings the assault rifle hanging on his back around front and grasps the trigger. At that exact moment, a large body flies through the smoke of the gas and hits Wayne chest high, sending him backwards. The man stays on top of Wayne as he hits the floor hard. Wayne loses the grip on his rifle as it slides across the floor about 10 feet. The man pulls Wayne's goggles off just as

Wayne is lifting him up with his leg and shoving him back. As the man regains his balance and prepares to attack again, Mike dives through the now open remains of the screen door and tackles him.

While Mike struggles to gain control over him, Wayne grabs his goggles and puts them back on just in time to see Mo Mower enter the smoke-filled room from the other side. Noticing he is about to open fire, Wayne covers the approximate 15 feet between him and Mo with a lunge and roll, followed by a sitting sidekick to Mo's midsection. Mo slams against the wall of the hall leading into the room. Wayne quickly gets to his feet and rushes Mo as he recovers from the kick. Mo blocks the next attack from Wayne and tries to get a shot off at him, but Wayne lifts his forearm just as he pulls the trigger and the shot goes up through the ceiling.

Wayne grabs Mo's gun arm while putting it in a reverse armlock, then, leaning downward, puts extreme resistant pressure on the muscles and bones of Mo's arm. The pain is excruciating as Mo screams and drops the gun but has enough presence of mind to counter the move by jumping and rolling over Wayne's shoulders, thus forcing a break in the hold. The move offers Mo an opportunity to grab Wayne's goggles as he falls to the ground on the other side of Wayne.

Wayne is familiar with the defensive move and lands on top of Mo, coming down hard on his chest with an elbow slam. Mo attempts to roll away, but Wayne follows quickly, keeping the attack in his favor. After some maneuvering and quick punch exchanges, both are able to regain their footing.

Even in the dark, they seem to sense the other's movement as Mo sweep kicks Wayne in midstep, causing him to come down hard against the wall and slide to the floor. As Wayne hits the floor, he coughs out the oxygen cylinder from his mouth. Mo, seeing his chance, retreats to a front room of the house with Wayne's night-vision goggles. Mike, left with no other choice, kills the one he is fighting and makes his way in the direction of Wayne.

Mike hears Wayne coughing from the tear gas that has taken over most of the house. Mike is next to him in seconds, sharing his oxygen until he locates Wayne's laying near his feet, along with Mo's gun. He hands them both to Wayne. Because of their small size, the cylinders can only carry about 5 minutes of oxygen. Their supply will be running out soon.

"He's got my goggles," a frustrated Wayne points out to Mike. "He'll be able to see us."

"Where is Taylor?" Mike asks.

Wayne tries to clear his head and focus on Mike's statement, realizing he has not seen her or Coffman since they came in. He shakes his head, acknowledging he does not know. Could they have gone out front and are now in the hands of the FBI? He stops short of believing that when he notices, through the darkness and smoke, that a door near them in the hallway is wide open.

He tells Mike to see if he can locate Mo in one of the front rooms as Wayne heads to the open door. Mike offers his night-vision goggles to Wayne, but he refuses them, knowing Mike will need them against Mo. Wayne reaches the door entrance and deliberately takes each step down into the dark basement. A slight creaking of one of the stairs causes Wayne to hesitate for a moment before continuing down. With Mo's gun and his own issued sidearm, Wayne has enough firepower, but that's not what worries him. He knows Coffman's training, so if he has Taylor, he will use her to his advantage.

He is soon at the bottom of the basement stairs and immediately notices the night sky coming in through the open back door that is under the deck. Wayne rushes through the door and out toward Rock Lake. Once out at the dock area, he looks up and down the lakefront. The night is bright from a full moon shining through a cloudless sky, but he is unable to notice anyone. He has to make a decision, right or left. A second later, he is running to the right, hoping that Coffman will try to make his way back to the expressway and find a way to stop a car.

Wayne picks up his pace as he runs along the lakefront before turning through an open yard and onto Shore Acres Road. If Coffman is dragging Taylor along, Wayne feels he should catch up quickly. Once on Shore Acres Road, Wayne looks to his left toward the West Madison Street entrance. He does not see anyone, so he starts to run up Shore Acres Road. Then, off in the distance, he hears the distinct sound of a boat motor. Wayne stops to listen. It doesn't take him long to analyze the odds of someone taking a boat out on a cool fall night for a pleasure ride. He quickly turns back to Rock Lake and the sound of the boat.

At the lakefront, he can see the faint dark image of a mid-size boat speeding north across the lake. With no time to lose, he runs back to his car in hopes of making it to the other side of the lake before the boat. At the car, he pulls his keys out while getting in. The car's tires screech as they leave a patch of rubber. Wayne turns the car around and heads north on West Madison Street. The road runs along the north area of Rock Lake to where the boat should make land.

Wayne pushes down on the gas pedal as he races along the road, slowing down only when he reaches a bend. Just seconds later, he looks out to the lake through a clearing of the trees and sees the boat coming closer as it continues on its path to the north end of the lake. It should be making land soon. Wayne sees a sign for Park Lane Road, a road that turns more toward the lakefront, so he takes it. Turning off his headlights, he proceeds more slowly down this road. With no trees on this route, he is able to watch the progress of the boat as it speeds across the lake.

Wayne has slowed the car to a crawl as he watches the boat continue its high rate of speed. He can't believe Coffman hasn't pulled back on the accelerator yet. He only has about 50 yards before land. Wayne sees the boat is going to hit hard on land about 300 yards away from him. He speeds up, parks only about 50 yards from where the boat will land, and gets out with both guns in hand. He sees the boat has not reduced its speed one bit as it crashes into the rocky bank of the lake and bounces a few feet up before coming to a stop some 10 feet on land.

Wayne rushes to the boat as the propellers continue to churn behind it. With guns continuing to move from side to side, he approaches the boat, but sees no one. Slowly he climbs on board and begins to search the upper and lower decks. When he reaches the cabin, he sees how the boat got where it is. The steering wheel, locked in place by a metal rod and tied off with a cord, is set to steer in one direction while the accelerator, pushed forward, is able to run on its own. Wayne jumps off the boat and races back to his car.

Back at the lake house, Garrett Coffman has gagged and tied Taylor in the basement, then made his way to the front of the house where he saw the two FBI agents laying in wait. With Wayne chasing an empty boat, Garrett is able to take his time with the two agents. It has been a while since he last used his Army Ranger training, but it is not something he has forgotten. As silently as a calm wind, Garrett stalks his targets with knife in hand. It is quick and quiet. Now the two agents lie where they once stood, breathing their last breaths. Garrett goes back around to the basement and passes Taylor as he silently walks up the steps to the first floor, remembering the step that creaked when he came down earlier.

Taking the last step, Garrett can hear Secret Service Agent Mike Peters questioning Mo Mower as to the whereabouts of Taylor and Coffman. Mo remains silent as Agent Peters threatens him with a bullet to the leg. It's the last thing Mike Peters does as Garrett moves in on him.

About a mile north, Wayne races his car south along West Madison Street, screeching the tires as he turns on to Shore Acres Road. He parks about 50 yards from the lakefront home and gets out of the car cautiously, even though he believes Coffman is probably miles from here now. He dreads telling Kathy and the President that he lost Taylor. He'll have to arrange for an All Points Bulletin since Coffman will be going into hiding.

He notices the power is still out at the house, as the front light is not working. He cannot see the FBI agents but assumes they are probably in the house with Mike. Wayne walks toward the house, looking around the area as he approaches. Within 20 yards of the house, he sees a slight movement over in a front bush of the house. Wayne stops his progress as he stares at the bush, trying to decide if it really moved or not. He crouches and quickly advances toward the bush. There is no additional movement, but he continues to it. At the bush, the darkness gives up a dark figure lying behind it. Wayne checks the FBI agent's vitals, but there is no sign of life now.

Wayne's senses kick in as he now realizes Coffman must have come back after sending the boat across the river. He looks around for the other agent and is able to make out another limp figure near the left front of the house. He quietly works his way over and confirms that the second FBI agent is also dead. He now fears for Mike. He decides to make his way around back to see if that door is still open. As he cautiously peers around the back corner of the house, he can see that the basement door is open.

Wayne moves to the door and looks in, but the darkness is too restrictive. He's unable to make anything out beyond 15 feet. He remembers where the stairs are, so he deliberately moves in that direction. He takes the stairs quietly, but as he reaches the fifth step, a distinct creak pierces the quiet. Wayne cringes as he stands on the offending step. He should have remembered that from earlier. Afraid to push off to the next step, he steps back, waits for a few seconds, then takes the next step up. At the top, he pokes his head through the door only enough to look to each side of the hall.

To the right is the room that he entered earlier this evening. To the left is where Mo ran after getting away during his fight with Wayne. That is also where Mike headed when Wayne left to try to catch Coffman. Wayne decides left is the way. He has only taken two steps down the hall when out of the darkness comes a voice he doesn't recognize but knows has to be Coffman.

"Come join us, Agent Mitchell. We've all been waiting for you," Garrett Coffman calls out.

Wayne pushes himself against the wall as much as he can and tries to see into the darkness of the end of the hall. He has guns drawn, his issued sidearm and the gun he took from Mo during the earlier fight. He also knows that he has knives attached to both ankles and a couple of tear gas canisters. What he doesn't have are the night-vision goggles and assault rifle. Both of which he figures Coffman now has. A thought comes to Wayne, and he slowly makes his way back to the basement door.

"Come on, Wayne," Coffman yells out. "Are you going to let this pretty young lady down? I'm sure she's hoping you've come all this way to save her. Or are you just looking for the ledger?"

Wayne stops at the top of the basement stairs, trying to remember which step squeaked. Remembering, he then slowly starts down.

"My sole purpose is to bring the girl back safely," Wayne answers. He knows he has to keep Coffman talking as he continues down the basement stairs.

"Yeah, right," Coffman responds sarcastically. "You're after the ledger, just like me. You just hope the girl will come with it. Isn't she a little young for you?"

Wayne stops his descent to the basement, "I'm nothing like you, Coffman. How does it feel to threaten the lives of the family of the co-pilot of Air Force 2 so that she would crash the plane killing the Vice-President, chief of staff, and everyone else on that plane?" Wayne taunts Coffman as he continues to the basement, avoiding the noisy step.

"So you know who I am and think you know something," Coffman acknowledges, "but all that is just guesswork. It's good guesswork, I'll give you that, but there's nothing you could have that would link any of what you said to anyone. I've been in business a long time for one reason: I don't leave a traceable trail on anything I do. So good luck with what you think you know and see if anyone will pursue it."

Wayne gets to the basement door, engages the deadbolt lock, then, as quickly as possible, heads back up the basement stairs just as Coffman finishes his statement.

Before reaching the top step, Wayne continues his questions: "How much did Osburn pay you to eliminate the chief of staff? It had to be a lot since it required you taking out the Vice-President too."

"Boy, you have been trying to connect the dots," Coffman says calmly.

"It had to be a lot more than what he paid to get rid of John Blackard," Wayne continues to press Coffman.

"My, oh my, you do think you know something," Coffman replies in his calm manner. "Well, if someone did pay me to do what you said, it would have been a lot for both. Tell me, Wayne, do you plan to talk to me until some reinforcements come to your rescue? I'll tell you what. I won't kill this pretty girl, but if you don't come out from behind that wall in the next few seconds, I'll be forced to put a bullet in her leg. Then if that doesn't work, her…"

Wayne listens intently, but not to what Coffman is saying. He's listening for the sound of the basement door trying to open. Just as Coffman was in the middle of his statement, the distinct sound of the basement door handle came up the stairs to Wayne's ears. He knows that has to be Mo Mower attempting to come up behind Wayne. This now leaves Garrett Coffman alone. Wayne knows he has less than a minute before Mo makes his way back around the house and through the front door.

Wayne, not trusting the gun he took from Mo, lays it down and keeps only his SIG Sauer P229 pistol in his hand. He has one chance at this, and he has to have a gun he trusts. Wayne takes a deep breath, runs, and dives into the front room just as Coffman is finishing his threat to Taylor.

Coffman, caught slightly off guard, sends a bullet that hits Wayne in the muscle of his left leg, passing through cleanly. Wayne's hope was that Coffman would take an unaimed shot. But with Coffman probably wearing Wayne's night-vision goggles, the darkness of the room was to Coffman's advantage. Wayne had to use the flash of Coffman's gun to locate accurately his position.

Before Wayne lands on the floor, he gets off a shot, aiming just above and to the right of where the gunshot flash came from. The bullet goes just past Taylor and hits Coffman around the right shoulder, not enough to kill him, but enough to cause him to recoil from the wound.

Wayne can now make out the dark figure as it stumbles back, letting go of Taylor. He then focuses on his next shot. Taking quick aim, he squeezes the trigger three more times and sends the bullets into the middle of Garrett Coffman's chest. The force of the shots lift Coffman off the ground and back against the far wall of the room, where the body ends up in a motionless heap. Taylor, gagged and with hands and feet tied, falls to the floor. Just then the front door explodes into the room as Mo Mower crashes through it.

Wayne reacts quickly, but his position leaves him in the direct path of Mower. All of a sudden, Wayne feels Mower land on top of him, along with a large piece of the door. Both men's weapons skid about the floor—one down the hall, the other over by Taylor. Wayne tries to roll but is pinned. Mower comes down with his fist onto the side of Wayne's head.

The blow stuns Wayne, but he retaliates with an elbow thrust to Mower's face, followed by a knee to his groin, then another elbow to the face. That combination weakens Mower enough to lose his advantage. Wayne cups his hands and with the heels hits Mower in the ears, causing a shockwave that punctures his eardrums. Mower grabs his head, trying to protect himself from additional blows as Wayne uses his leg to kick him off to the side so he can move out from under him.

Wayne stands and lands a solid sidekick to Mower's midsection that sends him across the room. He quickly advances after Mower, but sees that he has sent him next to Taylor. Mower, realizing his chance to regain the advantage, grabs the bound Taylor while reaching for the gun he sees near her and tries to bring both to him. She struggles as much as her bindings will allow. Wayne, seeing this, reaches down to his right ankle and, in one motion, grabs the knife attached to it and brings his arm up, releasing the knife. The throw is true as it passes just to the right of the struggling Taylor and hits Mower on the left side of his chest, going through the ribs and puncturing the heart.

Mo falls back, grabbing at the knife. With what little strength he has left, Mower pulls the knife from his chest and begins to throw it back at Wayne. Wayne reaches down with his left hand to grab his other knife, but then Mower's arm loses its strength and drops to his side and the knife falls harmlessly to the floor. Wayne walks over to him as he falls to the floor. He can see Mower trying to say something, but Wayne stays his distance. Blood seeps out of Mower's mouth as he coughs a little before his head slips to the side and his breathing stops.

Wayne rushes to Taylor and releases the binding around her arms and legs, then takes off the gag. Taylor grabs Wayne and begins to cry. Wayne wraps his arms around her.

"Are you all right Taylor?" Wayne asks anxiously.

"Yes," Taylor says between sobs.

While holding her, Wayne notices the lifeless body of Mike Peters lying on the floor on the other side of the room. He says a silent thank you to him as he hugs Taylor a little longer.

Twenty-three

Safe and Well

Wayne struggles to his feet with the help of Taylor. She immediately notices Wayne is hurt and takes him to a nearby couch to sit down. Taylor then leaves the room for a few minutes before coming back with some cloth to wrap the wound. Wayne sits back in the couch while Taylor tends to his leg. He then pulls his cell phone out of his pocket and calls the White House. Soon he is talking to the President.

"Mr. President, I have Taylor. She is safe and well."

"I cannot tell you how great that news is, Wayne," President Anders replies excitedly. "Let me get Kathy on the line."

A few seconds pass before Wayne hears Kathy, "Oh Wayne, thank you so much," Kathy talks through her tears.

"Let me put Taylor on," Wayne says as he hands his cell phone to Taylor.

"Hi, Mom," Taylor's voice excitedly greets her mother.

Wayne leans back in the couch, allowing mother and daughter some time to themselves. Soon Taylor says goodbye to her mother and hands the phone back to Wayne. Kathy again, between sobs, thanks Wayne for all he has done.

"I'll have her home soon, Kathy. Can you put the President back on?"

"Yes, Wayne." Kathy hands the phone back to President Anders.

"Sir, could you arrange to have a local MEDEVAC unit dispatched to Shore Acres Road in Lake Mills, Wisconsin?"

"Are you and Taylor all right?"

"Taylor is fine, but you can tell the unit that I have a bullet wound through the left leg. As much as I can tell, it passed through cleanly. Taylor's done a good job of wrapping it up." Wayne smiles at Taylor and she returns it. "Also, sir, I'm sorry to say we lost Mike Peters."

"I'm so sorry to hear that. I'll make arrangements to have the body brought back. See you both in a few hours." The President then hangs up.

Wayne then calls Brad Haler at FBI headquarters in Washington to tell him about the safe rescue of Taylor and the loss of agents Grafton and Kotewa. Wayne thanks him for all his help, emphasizing that Taylor's safe return could not have happened without his and the FBI's help. Brad thanks him and says he will inform the local office of what has happened there and to the agents. He assures Wayne that the FBI can handle the rest of the investigation and will round up anyone else associated with Garrett Coffman. Wayne says good-bye, then hangs up and motions to Taylor to sit next to him. Taylor settles in next to Wayne as they wait for the medical helicopter to arrive.

Less than 30 minutes later, they can hear the initial faint beating of propeller blades against the night air. The sound gradually gets louder until it reaches a near deafening level. Taylor gets up first and helps Wayne off the couch as the helicopter begins to descend on Shore Acres Road. The bright lights of the helicopter begin to shine through the windows of the home and light the way for Taylor to help Wayne out the door.

Slowly the two friends walk out into the cool night air as two medical team members rush to their side and help them the rest of the way to the helicopter. Once inside, the helicopter begins its trip back to Washington with Wayne and Taylor placed on gurneys. Doctors immediately start examining the two patients, but soon give Taylor the okay to move to a seat in the cabin if she wishes.

"No, I'd like to stay with my friend...if that's all right?" Taylor requests.

"No problem," the doctor says as Taylor sits up on her gurney to see Wayne better.

Wayne looks over at her and they both smile while the other doctor continues to work on Wayne's bullet wound. A few hours later, they are landing on the helipad at Bethesda Naval Hospital in Bethesda, Maryland. Taylor stays close to Wayne while his gurney moves from the helicopter into the hospital emergency ward. She continues to follow until he's wheeled into an operating room. There, she sits and waits outside the door.

Kathy, taken to the hospital by the Secret Service to await Taylor's arrival, appears from one of the waiting rooms. Taylor, crying, runs to her, and they hug tightly, as if to not allow another separation...ever. Kathy is the first to pull slightly away, but only to shower her with kisses and more hugs. After a few moments, they find seats next to each other near Wayne's operating room.

While waiting, they talk of what has happened over the last couple of days. Occasionally, anyone nearby would hear "Oh my" and "God was with you" as the two women relived experiences the other knew nothing about. Afterwards, they again reached for each other and continued to hold their embrace. Not too much later, one of the doctors comes out to tell them Wayne's surgery went well and he'll be walking normally again in no time.

"Can we see him?" Kathy asks.

"He's still under the anesthesia," the doctor replies. "It would be best to let him get some rest. His body has taken quite a beating."

He goes on to tell them that the hospital will keep Wayne overnight for observation, then release him in the morning. Both women thank the doctor, then Kathy leads Taylor over to where the Secret Service Agents are standing. They head to the limousine to ride back to the White House, where the President is anxiously awaiting their return.

At the White House, President Anders greets Taylor with a warm hug and leads her and her mother upstairs to the private quarters so they can relax and settle in for the night. Taylor will stay in the Lincoln

Bedroom, while her mother remains in the Queen's Bedroom across the hall.

The President mentions to Taylor, as he shows her the Lincoln Bedroom, "Amongst all the things Lincoln did, he also started the Secret Service, but back then their job was to stop counterfeiters, not protect politicians and their families."

"I'm very glad their job has changed," Taylor says with a smile.

The President smiles back. "Me too."

Before they all retire, the President, First Lady Claire and daughter Amy have the Bender women share a late meal with them. They listen to Taylor and Kathy tell of the amazing rescue that Wayne was able to accomplish and how their faith helped them deal with the past few days. The First Family can hardly eat a bite as they sit in silence listening to the amazing story. At the end, the President stands up and holds his glass for a toast.

"Let me say," the President begins, "that we are all exceedingly thankful no harm came to you and hope that the events of the past will be allowed to pass and that, with God's help, your lives will once again find happiness."

Everyone at the table nods in agreement and takes a sip from their respective glasses. The five finish their meal, then retire to their bedrooms. Kathy and Taylor sit in the Lincoln Bedroom for a while and talk, cry, and before separating, give a prayer of thanks. Kathy gives Taylor another hug as Taylor returns it even tighter. Kathy then kisses Taylor on the forehead and goes across the hall to her room. Taylor gets ready for bed and just before going to sleep says a prayer for Wayne.

The next morning the sun comes through the windows of the Lincoln Bedroom and settles on Taylor's face. Slowly her eyes open and she suddenly remembers where she is. Smiling, she gets out of bed and walks around the room. She had not taken time the night before to appreciate the room she is in. She tries to absorb all she sees: the paintings, the bed that Willie Lincoln passed away in, and over on the top of the writing desk, in a simple frame, a handwritten copy of the

Gettysburg Address in Abe Lincoln's own hand. All the history of Lincoln, his trials and suffering, is such a part of the room that it helps Taylor come to terms with what has happened to her family.

She goes over to her mother's room, wakes her, and brings her over to the Lincoln Bedroom so she too can feel it. In the morning light, the room takes on a glow that Kathy can feel. Taylor points out all the tragedy that the Lincolns had in their lives, yet somehow a feeling of peace comes from the room. The Bender women hold each other as they enjoy their moment with Lincoln.

Outside the room, they can hear the sounds of the White House staff doing their morning chores. The women realize they have to start getting ready. So with one last hug, they go about their morning ritual. This morning some appropriate clothing has arrived for Kathy and Taylor. The President had taken the liberty to have one of his staff pick out a selection for the women. Soon Kathy and Taylor are going through the variety of predominately black outfits, for today is Scott Bender's funeral, along with Vice-President Dave Charles'.

Washington is now preparing for one of the largest gatherings of world leaders—all of whom have come to pay their respects. The President has many responsibilities today, but he first makes time to meet with Lynn Charles and her daughters, Angela and Jessica. He then takes them up to the private quarters of the White House and has them stay with Kathy and Taylor until the funeral procession begins in a few hours. The President then leaves for his other appointments.

Outside, a black limousine pulls up to the front of the White House. About that same time, two sedans pull around to the West Wing entrance of the White House, dropping off four people who quickly enter the West Wing. A few minutes later, an ambulance pulls up behind the two sedans and Wayne Mitchell slowly swings his legs out. The driver runs around to the passenger side and hands Wayne a crutch that Wayne puts under his left armpit. Wayne thanks the man and slowly heads to the West Wing entrance.

Inside, everyone he passes enthusiastically greets Wayne. Wayne acknowledges all of them as he heads to the Oval Office. President Anders is at the door holding his hand out as Wayne grasps it.

"Thank you for all that you did, Wayne," the President says, then leads Wayne into the Oval Office.

Wayne immediately recognizes his friend, FBI Special Agent Brad Haler, as Brad walks over to shake Wayne's hand. The President then introduces the other three people in the room, who have stood to greet Wayne.

"Wayne," the President begins, "this is FBI Director Jeff Jenkins, House Speaker Sandi Elwell, and Senate Majority Leader Doug McDonald." Wayne shakes all their hands, then takes the seat right next to the President. The Speaker and Senate Leader are of the opposing party and have been brought in so there can be no misunderstanding on what is about to happen.

"Wayne," the President starts, "Director Jenkins and Special Agent Haler have briefed Sandi and Doug on what all was found in the wreckage of the Coffman building in Dayton, Maryland. They both agree that even though there are no names mentioned in any of the documents, there are strong links to former President Osburn. Add what you told me last night from the hospital concerning Agents Tim and Mike Peters' statements, they are in agreement with what will be done."

Wayne nods as the President gets up and walks to the door that leads to the corridor. "Go and get Osburn," he tells an aide.

The aide proceeds across the corridor to the windowless Roosevelt Room, where former President Osburn waits under the pretense that he will say something at the funeral. The aide knocks, then opens the door.

"Sir, the President will see you now," the aide says in a deadpan voice.

Shane Osburn gets up from the chair and follows the aide to the Oval Office. Shane is somewhat surprised to see who is there and that no one stands to greet him, but then thinks they are also going speak at the funeral.

The President hand-motions Shane to sit in the one empty chair across from the President.

"Shane, we have had a terrible thing happen to our country," the President states, "but we've only just found out that it was not an accident."

Shane Osburn's face stiffens as he continues to listen.

"During recent activities by Secret Service Agent Wayne Mitchell and FBI Special Agent Brad Haler, certain documents have come to light. Are you familiar with a person named Garrett Coffman?"

"No." Shane shakes his head in denial.

"That is odd, because we have statements from your former lead Secret Service Agent and your current lead agent that you are aware of that person," the President points out.

"I'm sorry; they must have their facts wrong," Shane counters defiantly.

"How far are you willing to go to prove that statement?" the President firmly demands.

"I don't understand," Shane responds less aggressively.

"The FBI is prepared to go after you for no less than conspiracy to commit first-degree murder...amongst a slew of other charges." The President stands while motioning to the others in the room, "But those of us in the room fear that such a proceeding could do irreparable damage, not only to the country, but to the office of the President of the United States."

"I had nothing to do with that plane crashing," Shane blurts out.

"Why would we be talking about a plane crash?" Wayne asks.

"Well, well, I just assumed because of the funeral," Shane stutters through his response.

"Don't test our patience any more, Shane," House Speaker Sandi Elwell scolds. "I and Senate Leader McDonald are the ones that are pressing not to send you to prison. Take what the President is about to tell you in silence or this meeting is over, and we will back all means to end your time as a free man."

Shane Osburn leans back in his chair as the President continues.

"Only the people in this room will know what we have decided this day. You will be under house arrest for the remainder of your life. You will have a new team of Secret Service Agents assigned to you on a rotating basis. None will be with you for more than three months. The media will have the story that a very rare and contagious disease has infected you—so contagious that it will prevent any future contact with anyone, including your wife and daughter. The Secret Service will monitor all calls in and out. An ambulance will be posted outside under the guise of taking you to a hospital. Instead, you will go to a private airport where a plane waits to take you to a secure location, to live out your life. Understand, if you attempt to fight this, you will be prosecuted to the full extent of the law and we will release all documents and videos linking you not only to the deaths of the people on Air Force 2, but also those who perished with Secretary John Blackard."

Shane Osburn is stunned. He does not understand how this could have happened. There was no detail left uncontrolled. How could they have anything that could implicate him? He knows this, but since there was no hesitation in their judgment against him, doubts begin to enter his confidence. Moreover, with his own party leaders against him, he could not hope to attempt a defense of himself. It would risk ruining for eternity his name and career accomplishments. He resigns himself to his fate.

The President walks over to the door leading to the corridor and motions for Osburn's new team of Secret Service Agents to come in and take the former president to his new life. After the agents escort Osburn out of the Oval Office, the others in the room exchange handshakes and begin to exit. President Anders asks Wayne to stay behind for a minute.

Twenty-four

The List

The President waits until the other people in the room leave, then walks over to Wayne. "I've made the arrangements for the bodies of Agents Tim and Mike Peters to go home. Their parents have been contacted and told of their heroic actions and will be here tomorrow to take their sons back home for burial next weekend. I plan to go and wondered if you would like to join me?"

"Yes sir, I would like that."

"I took your advice," the President adds, "and had the black box retrieved from Air Force 2. It is being analyzed now."

"Sir, I would respectfully request that what is found remains confidential."

"Yes, I agree. It would be terrible for Ingrid's family to have to suffer anymore. What a terrible thing she was forced to do to save her children. I'd hate to have to make that choice," the President confides.

Wayne agrees as the two men head out the door to be a part of the funeral procession that will be starting soon.

"Sir, have you gotten the list from the lockbox?" Wayne asks as they make their way down the hall toward the door that will take them to the main floor of the White House.

"No, not yet, Wayne," President Anders replies. "I didn't want to bring it up while Kathy was worrying about her daughter's safety. I will approach her about helping me with that once things settle down and

Taylor goes back to school."

"I agree, sir," Wayne says as the two men approach the area of the West Wing where the offices of the chief of staff and the Vice-President are. They stop and pay silent homage to the two men who gave their lives serving their country, then continue on to the main White House.

The President has arranged for many of the dignitaries to come to the White House to pay their respects to the families of Vice-President Charles and chief of staff Bender. As Wayne and President Anders enter the first floor of the White House residence, which connects to the ground floor of the West Wing, they meet many of the White House staff eager to greet Wayne and shake his hand. Wayne, a little overwhelmed by all the attention, still manages to acknowledge each person as he struggles with his new crutch. They then take the elevator up to the private quarters on the third floor.

As the elevator doors open onto the third floor, Wayne sees Taylor and Kathy waiting. Both smile at seeing their friend. As he and the President exit the elevator, the two women each take a side of Wayne, kiss him on the cheek, and then help him to the Oval Yellow Room where Lynn Charles and daughters, Angela and Jessica, are waiting with First Lady Claire and daughter Amy.

The families sit and talk for a while until the President's senior advisor, Diana Woodworth, appears at the entrance to the room and informs everyone that it is time to go downstairs. They all slowly rise from their chairs and take the Grand Staircase down to the Entrance Hall where the receiving line will form for the friends, relatives, and dignitaries to pay their respects before the funerals.

Televised around the world, the funerals for David Charles and Scott Bender were an emotional event for everyone as the two families used each other for support and showed their strength to the world. During the proceedings, the media mentioned that former president Shane Osburn was at Bethesda Naval Hospital after an ambulance rushed him from the White House and then later transferred to an unknown location for treatment.

After the funerals, the families returned to the White House for one more night before saying their good-byes. Wayne was supposed to stay home and rest for a few days after the funerals, but the President heard he had returned to work early so he summoned him to the Oval Office….

When Wayne arrives, the President greets him and offers a seat next to his desk. The President walks around the desk to his chair and sits as Wayne takes the crutch from under his arm and leans it against the chair before sitting.

"Wayne, I've talked with Kathy and she has kindly agreed to go to the EagleBank branch and check the lockbox to see if Scott's ledger is there. I was going to send my new lead Secret Service Agent to accompany her, but if you wouldn't mind…?"

Wayne smiles. "Sir, I'd be happy to go with Kathy."

"Thank you, Wayne. I'm having a car bring her here for lunch first, then you two can head over to the bank. She should be here soon. She and Taylor have been staying in their guesthouse while a construction crew repairs the main house. It was good they stayed here during those first few days; it gave my men time to go and clean up. Coffman must have taken the bodies since they informed me there were none at the residence."

"That makes sense," Wayne concurs. "He wouldn't have wanted to leave anything or anyone that could tie him to what happened there."

A few moments later, there is a knock on the door to the Oval Office and the President's secretary tells him that Kathy Bender is arriving.

A few moments later Kathy enters the Oval Office, and the President's secretary tells the three that lunch is about to be served in the Dining Room. The President's dining room is just past his study, so it's just a short walk for them.

During lunch, the conversation is light and at times funny as they try to remember the good times. The President then asks about Taylor.

"She boarded a plane back to Wisconsin this morning. She should be landing in the next hour," Kathy answers.

"I'm sorry I didn't say good-bye," Wayne says with a regretful tone.

"She told me she'd be calling you in a couple of days," Kathy explains. "She thought you would still be resting."

"He was supposed to be," the President adds.

The three laugh as they finish their lunch. The President mentions to Kathy that Wayne will be joining her this afternoon if that would be all right.

"I would enjoy that, Mr. President," Kathy responds and smiles at Wayne.

The President then gets up from the table, saying he has other commitments so must go. "This is the key that your husband had for the lockbox at EagleBank," the President explains as he hands the key to Kathy.

Kathy nods and takes the key from the President.

"Thank you for helping me with this," the President says as he grasps her hand, then leaves the room.

Wayne puts his crutch back under his arm as he and Kathy walk out to the West Wing entrance, where a car and driver are waiting for them. With a change in etiquette, Kathy helps Wayne into the car before the driver helps her in.

About 800 miles away, Taylor's plane has landed. As she leaves the plane, she looks for her roommate, who is to pick her up. She walks a few more yards before she hears her name yelled. Turning her head in the direction of the voice, she sees Debbie Lawrence, her roommate, waving to her. Taylor waves back, then heads over to Debbie.

"So good to see you," Debbie tells Taylor as they hug each other.

"I'm more glad to be back than you'll ever know," Taylor replies as they both smile and start walking out of the terminal.

Back in Washington, it's only a short drive to the DuPont Circle branch of EagleBank. When Kathy and Wayne's car pulls into the parking lot, the driver gets out and helps Kathy first, then goes over to the other side of the car to help Wayne. Once inside the bank an employee greets them and asks how the bank can be of service.

"My name is Kathy Bender, and I'd like to get into my husband's lockbox," Kathy explains. "He passed away last week, and I need to check its contents. I have a copy of the death certificate if you need to see it."

"That won't be necessary, Mrs. Bender," the bank employee answers. "The White House called and said that you would be coming. Please follow me." The employee leads Kathy and Wayne to the back part of the bank, where the lockboxes are.

At the University of Wisconsin, Taylor is now in her dorm room with Debbie, unpacking her suitcase. The two girls are putting Taylor's clothes away when Debbie leaves for a minute. When she returns, she is holding a bunch of mail.

"I picked up your mail like you asked," Debbie says as she hands the stack of mail to Taylor.

In the EagleBank branch, the employee takes Kathy and Wayne into the vault that houses the lockboxes and has Kathy sign the entrance register. She then takes Kathy's lockbox key, puts it into the keyhole of the lockbox, then inserts the master key into the adjoining keyhole and turns the keys simultaneously. The door to the lockbox opens. The employee leaves Kathy and Wayne in the lockbox room alone to examine the contents.

In the dorm room, Taylor takes the mail from Debbie and looks at it. Just your normal mail for the most part, except for one item—a slightly larger piece of mail with a few more stamps on it. Taylor lays it down on her bed with the other mail while she and Debbie finish unpacking her suitcase.

"Thanks, Deb."

"No problem," Debbie responds. "You know, though, a funny thing happened when I went to pick up your mail a few days ago. A guy in the student union mentioned he had seen you the day before and was surprised you were back on campus. I just figured he was mistaken."

Taylor smiles, remembering that someone had recognized her in the student union and had even talked to her, "Yeah, he must have seen someone who looks like me." Taylor decides it's too complicated to try to explain what really happened now…maybe another time.

After they have all of Taylor's clothes back where they belong, Debbie asks Taylor if she would like to share a pizza.

"Sure, that would be great."

Debbie leaves to make the call as Taylor looks down at the mail on her bed, particularly the unusual-sized one. She reaches down and picks it up, holding it for a moment before deciding to open it. She tears open the top of the tan colored envelope and pulls out what is inside.

At EagleBank, Kathy reaches into the lockbox sleeve and pulls out the lockbox as Wayne stands off to the side. He is there to retrieve the list, not to intrude on anything personal. Kathy begins to extract items and lay them on the table next to her. Each item is something from Scott's office, but not from the government part. She pulls out a signed baseball, a couple of signed baseball cards, and some letters from the people who signed the baseball and cards. She then pulls out a couple of presidential pens, some items with AIR FORCE ONE embossed on them, along with some signed pictures of Scott posing with a number of celebrities. They are things important to Scott Bender, but not what they're looking for.

Wayne shakes his head, realizing he has hit another dead-end.

"I'm sorry, Wayne," Kathy softly says.

"It must have been with Scott on the plane," Wayne concludes.

After leaving the bank, the driver drops Wayne back at the White House before taking Kathy back home. Before Wayne gets out of the car, he and Kathy make plans to meet for dinner in a couple of weeks when his leg is a little better. He then walks into the West Wing and heads to the Oval Office. Wayne waits in the corridor outside until the President is able to see him.

It's only a few minutes before the door to the Oval Office opens, and the President brings Wayne in.

"Well, do you have it?" President Anders anxiously asks.

"I'm sorry, Mr. President, but it was not there."

Frustrated, the President returns to his desk and sits in his chair.

"He must have had it on the plane with him," Wayne tries to explain. "In a way it makes sense since he'd been using it to blackmail people. He probably felt he had to keep it close just in case he had to prove what he had."

The President leans back in his chair, his expression now more calm. "That does make some sense. I mean, we've searched every conceivable place it could be, haven't we?"

"Yes sir," Wayne replies.

"Well, that's that." The President then gets up from behind his desk and walks over to Wayne. "I want you to go home and take some real time off. I don't want to hear that you are back at work again until next week. Are we in agreement on that?"

Wayne nods emphatically.

"Okay then, get out of here," the President says and gives him a playful nudge toward the door as he holds it open for him.

Wayne, with his crutch under his left arm, makes his way back to his car. His mind, though, cannot help but go over all that has happened the last week. Thinking back on it all, he agrees, he really should take some time off. He reaches his car and takes the crutch from under his arm and tosses it over onto the passenger side, then gets into the car.

A few moments more and he is pulling out of the White House drive and heading home. Just as he is about to turn on the radio, something pops into his thoughts. It was something Garrett Coffman said just before Wayne killed him: *"You are after the ledger, just like me."*

Why would Coffman say that when it should have been obvious Wayne was there to save Taylor? Unless Taylor had truly led Coffman to believe she had it. Wayne now remembers where the FBI agents said they saw Coffman—in the student union. If Wayne's college memory is correct, then he knows why they were at the student union. That's where the mailroom is, but nothing had arrived yet.

"Taylor told Coffman that she mailed the ledger to her college mail address," Wayne says aloud. "That really is why they went to the University of Wisconsin."

Wayne laughs as he remembers thinking she might have said something like that in order to buy some time, but in actuality, she really did have the list all along. Wayne continues on his way home, planning to contact Taylor tomorrow and see if he can talk her into giving him the list. He will explain in detail what it is so she can understand why the President needs it back. For now, though, he is going home to rest and watch some golf on TV.

In Taylor's dorm room, Debbie comes back in and sees Taylor with a book. "Some new reading material?" Debbie asks.

Taylor hesitates, then decides to confess. "It's my dad's *Little Black Book*. I came across it when I was going through his desk after he died. It has a bunch of women's names in it."

"You're kidding!" Debbie says in disbelief.

"No, I wanted to hide it from my stepmom. We have just started getting along and I was afraid if she saw that my father had a book of women, it would hurt our relationship from then on. What's even worse is that so many people knew about my dad's *Black Book.* Some, I'm afraid, wanted to use it to ruin my dad's name and were even willing to kill for it."

"Oh Taylor, you poor thing." Debbie reaches over to console her.

"And that guy you mentioned," Taylor continues, "really did see me. The men who wanted to harm my father's name had brought me back here to get this book. Luckily, we got back after the mailroom was closed."

"You know what you should do? You should shred it," Debbie advises. "That way no one will ever be able to use it against your family."

"You know you're right," Taylor enthusiastically agrees.

"There is a shredder in the common room at the end of the hall," Debbie informs her friend.

"Let's go," Taylor says as she gets up and heads out of her room with Debbie following close behind.

At the end of the hall is the common room, where the residents of that floor of the dorm can gather and do homework or just socialize. It has a soda and snack machine, a microwave, and in the corner, a paper shredder.

Taylor walks directly to the shredder and begins to tear pages from the *Little Black Book* and feed them into the shredder. The whirring sound of the shredder blades is continuous as Taylor sends page after page into them. A few moments later, The List is no longer.

EAGLE LOST

CRAIG D. MCLAREN

A deadly threat
is about to be unleashed…

During his re-election campaign, the President of the United States decides to sneak away for a quiet weekend of fishing. Only three people know of his whereabouts—including Secret Service Agent Wayne Mitchell, assigned to protect the President on that trip.

When the President is kidnapped, Mitchell races against the clock to find the world leader…and stumbles upon a conspiracy dating back to the Cold War era that now has grown into a cataclysmic threat to all Americans.

*An action-laden political thriller
that will make you think,* What if…?

www.oaktara.com

About the Author

CRAIG D. MCLAREN is a retired bank president who dreamed of being a Secret Service Agent when he read his first James Bond novel in the early 60s.

"I even looked into interviewing for such a position while attending Carthage College in the 70s, before my graduate studies at the University of Wisconsin," Craig says. "My desire to be an author started from many experiences associated with what I saw as a president of a bank, when I dealt with government officials. It all came together when I saw something in a fictional book about our President and government that concerned me and I asked myself, *What if...?*"

Craig McLaren's goal is to write believable novels that will be interesting to all—from young teens to adults. *The List* is Book Two in The Secret Service: Agent Wayne Mitchell series. Don't miss Book One, *Eagle Lost.*

Craig enjoys hearing from his readers. You may email him at:
craigmclaren7@mchsi.com

For more info:
www.oaktara.com

CPSIA information can be obtained at www.ICGtesting.com
Printed in the USA
LVOW13s1719300514

387959LV00002B/359/P